A BELOW STAIRS MYSTERY COLLECTION II

VOLUME 2

BELOW STAIRS MYSTERIES

JENNIFER ASHLEY

JA / AG PUBLISHING

CONTENTS

A MEASURE OF MENACE

CHAPTER 1

October 1883

"Lord Clifford has arrived," Mr. Davis, the Mount Street house's butler, announced as he entered the kitchen.

I glanced up in surprise from my worktable, where papers, my notebook, and several cooking tomes were strewn about me. I'd seized the opportunity of having no family in the house to go over my recipes for the next social Season, which would begin in January. I'd be expected to come up with a myriad of meals for whatever gatherings my mistress, Mrs. Bywater, had planned, and I wanted to be prepared.

"I beg your pardon?" I demanded of Mr. Davis.

The Bywaters had taken Lady Cynthia, their niece, with them to their country house in Somerset to enjoy crisp autumn weather and the shooting. I knew neither Mr. nor Mrs. Bywater would actually creep through wet grass to aim a shotgun, but they would happily eat whatever their friends bagged. Mrs. Bywater was one for brisk walks but no exertion beyond that.

Cynthia, I imagined, would suffer continuous ennui. While she delighted in vigorous activity, she was not keen on her aunt's and uncle's rather vapid acquaintances in the country.

They'd left most of the staff behind, except Mr. Bywater's valet and Sara, the upstairs maid who doubled as a lady's maid. Mrs. Bywater had decided that anyone else would be too much expense in train tickets.

We were to keep the house in order and well stocked for the Bywaters' return later in the winter. I'd half expected Mrs. Bywater to insist we take less pay, as the family would not be in residence, but I suspected Cynthia had prevented that.

"Lord Clifford asked that I make up a room for him," Mr. Davis answered, clearly annoyed. He'd wanted this quiet time to inventory the wine, and Lord Clifford had the habit of pinching bottles from the cellar. "He tells me that he requires only a light repast for supper."

I gazed around the empty kitchen in dismay. The dresser held a small box of aging potatoes and a few herbs. A pot of stock slowly burbled on the back of the stove as always. I'd retained enough in the larder to feed the staff, but there was little more than that.

"Oh, does he just?" I all but snapped.

"Indeed. Mrs. Redfern is settling him in, being very civil."

Which meant that Mrs. Redfern was as annoyed as the rest of us.

Lord Clifford was Lady Cynthia's father. Mr. Bywater's sister had married him, connecting the Bywaters' ordinary but well-off family with penniless aristocrats.

Lord Clifford was a rogue of the first water, who had more or less swindled his way into his title. By now, all other claimants had passed away, so he really was the Earl of Clifford, but at one point, he had definitely not been first in line.

I rather liked the rapscallion, who had an absent-minded kindness in him, and he had suffered the loss of two of his children. But whenever Lord Clifford appeared, trouble soon followed.

"Well, his repast will be *very* light." I slammed my notebook shut and tossed down my pencil. "I can nip out to the market, but I doubt I will find anything at this hour." It was late afternoon, and anything good in the markets would be gone.

Mr. Davis, having no reply to this, stalked from the kitchen and continued down the passageway to his butler's pantry. The banging door sent a cold draft that fluttered my papers at the table.

I tidied my books and notes before I rose and snatched up my coat and basket. I ordered Tess, who'd just come in but lingered in the scullery to chat with Elsie, the scullery maid, to start slicing the potatoes. I'd given Tess the afternoon out, as we weren't busy and I'd wanted the time to work on my menus, so she was bubbling with good spirits.

"Right you are, Mrs. H.," she said cheerily, sailing into the kitchen.

"Put them in a bowl of cold water, so they won't turn brown," I instructed before I charged out of the scullery door, trying not to mutter under my breath about unheeding lordships who couldn't be bothered to send word ahead.

The cool air as I ascended to the street calmed me somewhat—it was a lovely autumn evening—but Lord Clifford had caught us at a decided disadvantage.

However, I, a mere cook, could not turn out an aristocrat from his daughter's home or refuse to feed him. If I dug in my heels and informed him he'd have to find a meal elsewhere, I'd soon be out a post, and when all is said and done, I am a practical woman.

Also, I was a bit curious as to why Lord Clifford had abruptly turned up. Mr. Davis had made no mention of his wife accompanying him, or Lady Cynthia either. Why he wasn't at his country estate engaged in shooting fowl like the Bywaters and every other gentleman in Britain was a mystery.

The greengrocer in Oxford Street had slim offerings, as I'd suspected. I filled my basket with a few small cabbages, choosing those with the fewest dark spots, some additional potatoes that weren't too soft, and carrots that were the crispest of the lot.

I had some salt pork in the larder, but that was hardly fit for an earl, so I stepped to the nearest meat market for sausages the butcher hurriedly wrapped for me. He was about to close up shop and not happy he had one last customer to wait upon. I thanked him sweetly, paid over the coins, and headed home.

Once Tess and I had chopped everything, I put the vegetables and sausages together in a pan along with the potatoes that Tess had already prepared, stirring vigorously with my metal spoon to relieve my pique.

When the meal was complete, I sent it up with a few homemade buns, hot from the oven. I always had fresh dough handy so I could bake what I needed to. For sweet, Lord Clifford would have to make do with cheese and a few sliced figs. Mr. Davis raised his brows over the offering, no doubt worrying about what wine would go with it.

He sighed and took himself upstairs, his stiff back telling me he hadn't recovered from his irritation.

The staff were happy to tuck into the remainder of the dish, rounded out with the salt pork and more buns. I ate with them, though I usually took my meals alone or with Mrs. Redfern. Someone needed to keep an eye on the under servants—the footmen in particular were wont to be too boisterous. Mr. Davis and Mrs. Redfern were upstairs waiting on Lord Clifford, so it fell to me to be their minder.

Mr. Davis returned before I'd finished my repast.

"Lord Clifford requests to see you, Mrs. Holloway," he announced in his haughty butler's tones. "Right away, if you please."

I dabbed my mouth with my napkin then stood and carried my plate to the kitchen. I set it on the table and laid my napkin over it, indicating I'd return. I was still hungry and did not want the others to pinch my food.

"He gobbled up his meal fast enough," Mr. Davis said to me once we were in the passageway. "Never seen a man eat so intensely. Didn't make much conversation, only demanded more wine once he'd slurped down the first glass."

"And wishes to see me?" I asked with misgivings. I gestured toward the back stairs. "Shall we?"

Mr. Davis shook his head. "He stressed that you should come alone. Which suits me. I'd like some of that supper myself."

"I have a plate warming for you on the stove," I told him.

Mr. Davis sent me a grateful nod and made his way into the kitchen, finished with Lord Clifford. I dropped my grease-stained apron into the laundry room as I passed it, smoothed my hair, and climbed the stairs to the main house.

It was very quiet with the family gone. I missed Lady

Cynthia, who liked to bound down to the kitchen and chatter away, regaling me with tales of her unconventional friends. Her conversation these days was full of Mr. Thanos, a clever but shy young man who lectured at the Polytechnic in Cavendish Square. I was pleased with her interest.

I entered the large dining room to find Lord Clifford by himself—Mrs. Redfern must still be busy opening up rooms for him. He was seated at the head of the table, in Mr. Bywater's place. The table, even without its extra leaves, held eight, and Lord Clifford looked small and alone in the vast space.

Lord Clifford's hair was a light shade of brown touched with gray that receded from a high forehead. He'd let his moustache and sideburns grow thicker since I'd last seen him, possibly to compensate for losing more hair on the top of his head.

He shoveled in a last mouthful of the meal I'd prepared for him, wiped his lips on the linen napkin, and beamed at me, though his smile held some sadness.

"An excellent repast, Mrs. Holloway. I should have expected no less. What did you call this dish?" Lord Clifford tapped his empty but sauce-streaked plate with his fork.

"Bubble and squeak," I answered. "I am afraid there was little else to feed you."

"Bubble and what?" The earl chuckled. "Excellent. I must have our own cook learn to prepare it."

"I'm certain she already knows, your lordship. It is a common dish below stairs, made with leftover cabbage, potatoes, and sausage or bacon. Except I bought most everything fresh tonight and added some carrots for body."

"Well, it was excellent, whatever you call it." Lord Clifford pushed the plate away. "Do sit down, Mrs. Holloway. I need to speak to you."

I curtsied stiffly. "That would be quite inappropriate, your lordship."

"Pish-tosh. There is no one here. It's why I sent old Davis and Mrs. Redfern away. I have something I wish to tell you, most urgently, and no one else can overhear."

With one hand, he shoved out the chair next to him. I contemplated it, then moved down the table to the chair above the one he wished me to take and conceded to sit in that. It did feel good to let my legs bend, but I held my hands in my lap and kept my back straight.

"Very well." Lord Clifford breathed the words in exasperation. "I came to you because I heard my nuisance in-laws were out of the house. I'm in a bit of a bind, Mrs. Holloway, about a very delicate matter."

I kept my face impassive, not wishing to betray the alarm that filled me at his every word. "What is this delicate matter?" I made myself ask.

Lord Clifford traced designs on the tablecloth with the handle of his fork. A few drops of dark sauce fell on the linen, but I said nothing about it.

"You see, I owed a chap a powerfully large sum of money," he said after a few moments of silence.

Oh, dear. Lord Clifford could be a bit of a confidence trickster, but he also, according to Cynthia, sometimes wagered heavily or became enmeshed in dealings he could not afford to be, and so had to borrow money to get out of them.

"A moment, your lordship," I said, as his precise wording struck me. "You said *owed*. Do you not owe this man any longer?"

"No." Lord Clifford drew a sharp breath. "Because he's dead. Bashed on the head, or knifed, or something, a few days ago." He dropped the fork to the plate with a clatter and fixed me with a desperate gaze. "Some think I did it. I did not. I need you, Mrs. Holloway, and that clever fellow, McAdam, to prove I am innocent."

CHAPTER 2

I sat still while dismay bordering on panic washed through me. Lord Clifford had the habit of getting himself into scrapes, sometimes dangerous ones, and I did not doubt that what he told me was true.

In my dim understanding of our justice system, a lord wasn't tried at the Old Bailey like the rest of us. He was expected to stand before his peers in the House of Lords and hope he hadn't made enough enemies among them to be condemned.

Even if he weren't convicted, the shame of the earl standing trial would be a blow for his wife and daughter, yet another scandal Lady Cynthia would carry for the rest of her life. The Shires family had been through several terrible ones already.

Lord Clifford regarded me piteously. He must be desperate if he'd decided the best help he could find was his daughter's cook and that cook's beau.

I told myself to approach the problem in the calm and sensible way I would any troubles below stairs.

"Did you actually see this dead man?" I asked trying to keep my voice steady. "I believe not, as you have no idea how he was killed."

"It is not that simple." Lord Clifford regained some of his arrogant impatience. "I did visit Mobley earlier that day—this past Sunday, it was. I'd arranged the meeting with him, even though his shop is shut on Sundays, as though he's a pious man." He scoffed. "As I say, I owed him quite a sum, and I asked him to give me longer to fetch it for him. We argued—loudly. I stormed away, and I am afraid a number of people saw me. Hiram Mobley's place of business is in the Strand. The road is quite busy, even on a Sunday, and the appearance of an earl in his carriage with his coat of arms is noticed."

"You took your own carriage to meet with this insalubrious person?" I blurted before I could stop myself.

Lord Clifford blinked. "Of course. How else was I to move about Town? My coachman drove me here all the way from St. Albans. I saw no reason for him to put his feet up while I charged about in a hansom."

"A hansom might have been more discreet, your lordship."

"I was not trying to hide from anyone." Lord Clifford shrugged. "I borrowed the money, fair and square, and I meant to pay it back. I thought I'd have plenty to give Mobley, well within the allotted time, but I've had rotten luck, is all."

Lord Clifford often had rotten luck. "Did you lose it on a horse?" I asked.

His eyes widened. "On the gee-gees? No, no. Horses are notoriously unreliable unless one has an informant in the stables or can somehow have a sure winner nobbled. But that's cruel to the beasts, so I stay away from it."

My hands tightened in my lap. "Perhaps you should tell me exactly why you borrowed the money, your lordship."

"I had to prove that I could put up my half, didn't I?" Lord Clifford's gaze willed me to tell him he'd been in the right. "He'd never have agreed if I hadn't shown him the money. Let the dog see the rabbit, eh?"

"*Who* wouldn't have agreed?" I asked in perplexity. "The bookmaker?"

"What bookmaker?" Lord Clifford was as bewildered as I was. "I never saw a bookmaker. I told you, this wasn't about horses. Or any other sort of wager."

"Then what on earth was it about?" I commanded in exasperation.

"Steamships, of course," Lord Clifford answered, as though this was reasonable. "Investing in a company of them, specifically. One a friend owns. It was an excellent dodge, and I could not resist. But it went wrong when old Dougherty refused to commit to the full share. We had him on the hook —oh, so beautifully—and then he said he didn't think steamships were a good investment after all. We'd doubled his first, smaller stake, but he refused to give us a larger one. He'd decided to put all his money in railroads through the wilds of Canada. Idiot. Someone is fleecing him good and proper."

My hands tightened further as I sorted through his convoluted tale. "You are saying you borrowed money to convince this Mr. Dougherty to invest in a steamship company?"

Lord Clifford tapped the table with the flat of his fingers. "You have it, Mrs. Holloway. I met old Dougherty at one of my clubs. He is rolling in riches, is the man. A nabob. I wish I could have been a nabob rather than an earl. I'd quite enjoy all that money, and I don't care much for what people think of me. I truly thought gaining a title would make me filthy rich and give my wife a bit of a lark, but it has not turned out the way I thought at all." He ended on a sorrowful note.

"Why was it important for you to have cash?" I steered him back to the point. "If Mr. Dougherty was the one investing in the company, why did *you* need money?"

"Well, he didn't know my friend Jacoby had set up the scheme, did he?" Lord Clifford's expression softened into a self-satisfied one. "I didn't let on I knew Jacoby at all. I suggested that both Dougherty and I begin with a small investment, as it was a good venture I'd heard about. An equal amount from both of us. I had to produce my share and show it to Dougherty, or he wouldn't have gone through with the preliminary investment."

I steeled myself. "What was the amount?"

"Ten thousand guineas." Lord Clifford winced. "I owed fifteen on it by the time Mobley turned up his toes. Would have been even more, had he lived."

"Fifteen thousand … "

My dismay returned. The dead Mr. Mobley must have been an unscrupulous moneylender who charged exorbitant rates of interest. These sorts of men would lend to anyone, but they expected to be paid back on time and turned dangerous if they were not.

When I was a girl, a moneylender had set up shop around the corner from Bow Lane where I'd grown up. My mother had never let me walk past his place, as various ruffians the moneylender employed would lurk outside it. I reasoned that they'd not be interested in a skinny lass rushing by, as I could never possibly owe them money, but I'd heeded my mother's warning.

"It would have been worth it and easy to repay," Lord Clifford said mournfully. "*If* Dougherty hadn't pulled out. He cheated us out of that money, blast the man."

Or, Dougherty had tumbled to the fact that Lord Clifford and his friend were trying to swindle him and had prudently walked away.

"You said you'd doubled Mr. Dougherty's investment," I continued. "Which means your stake would have doubled as well, would it not? Couldn't you have used that to pay back the moneylender?"

Lord Clifford regarded me with exaggerated patience. "No, Mrs. Holloway. We gave the money *I* borrowed to Dougherty. We had to. To convince him that a larger investment would be sound."

"I see." I wanted to shake the man. "You were tricking him into thinking that his investment had doubled, when you hadn't invested the money at all."

Lord Clifford tapped the side of his nose. "Now, you understand."

Oh, good heavens. "Is your friend's steamship company even real?"

"Of course it is. Jacoby's offices are in Wellclose Square, near the London Docks. He's got stake in a ship and everything. Only, the income is not what he'd wish. We thought we'd spark it a bit."

By cheating an honest man out of ten thousand pounds. But the scheme had failed, putting Lord Clifford deeply in debt to a moneylender who was no better than a swindler himself.

I drew a deep breath. "If this false dividend had

persuaded Mr. Dougherty to give you still more money, what would you have done with it?"

"Jacoby was going to put it into his shipping company, of course. The investment would have been bound to pay off eventually, and Dougherty would see *some* return for it. Maybe not the riches Jacoby had claimed, but something. We could have strung him along for a while."

I briefly wondered how Cynthia, who could be so wise, had sprung from such a gullible parent.

"Would Dougherty *ever* have seen any money, your lordship?" I pinned him with my no-nonsense gaze.

"Why not? He and I both stood to gain from the larger investment, and Jacoby promised my money would come back to me five-fold, if not in the vast sums we'd promised Dougherty ..."

As I continued to stare at him, Lord Clifford frowned, and his fingers began to twitch.

Then his face crumpled entirely, and he fell back against his chair. "Oh, bloody hell. Mrs. Holloway," he said limply. "What have I done?"

He'd provided himself a motive for murdering the moneylender, was what he'd done. Mr. Jacoby obviously had planned to cheat Lord Clifford as well as Mr. Dougherty, roping Lord Clifford in by pretending to be such a good friend. Lord Clifford might have borrowed still more money and been in a tight spot indeed. Mobley's death had possibly relieved him of this.

"I'm not certain what you believe I can do, your lordship," I said after a time. "Catching whoever murdered the money-lender is the business of the police."

"Good Lord, I can't have the police mucking about in my

business. You have no need to solve the murder entirely, Mrs. Holloway. Only to prove that *I* didn't kill the man."

I decided not to point out that both tasks would perforce be one and the same. "I understand." I ran through various ways I could help at all, then emitted a sigh. "Very well. I will see what I can do."

The utter gratitude with which Lord Clifford beheld me almost made me soften to him. Almost.

"And please, please, whatever you do, do not tell my wife," Lord Clifford begged. "Or Cynthia. *She'd* rake me over hot coals. Promise me you'll keep them out of this."

I had no intention of distressing Lady Clifford or Lady Cynthia with this mess. "I will do my best."

"Thank you." Lord Clifford rested his elbows on the table, his face in his hands. "Thank you, Mrs. Holloway. You are an angel of mercy."

———

I LEFT LORD CLIFFORD STEWING IN HIS REALIZATION THAT HE had borrowed a large sum from a crooked moneylender to give to his equally crooked friend. It was clear to me that Mr. Jacoby had planned to fleece Lord Clifford not only out of the ten thousand, but out of whatever Mr. Dougherty had come up with for the full investment. Lord Clifford ought to bless Mr. Dougherty for turning away before Mr. Jacoby pulled the two men deeper into his schemes.

I wondered if Lord Clifford could be forgiven the debt to the moneylender, since the moneylender was now deceased. Mobley's heirs might want to be repaid, of course, but once the nature of Mobley's business was exposed to the police, the heirs perhaps wouldn't be able to collect. But there was no telling.

I descended to the kitchen before Mr. Davis decided to come hunt for me. As far as he was concerned, I'd only gone to the dining room to receive praise for my meal, but I'd been some time about it.

Tess, still exuberant from her unexpected holiday, started to clean up supper and prepare breakfast, refusing my offer of sending her to bed early. She was too keyed up, she said, and would never sleep.

"Hard work helps a body rest, don't it?" Tess asked as she scraped food scraps into a basket. She ruined this virtuous statement by adding, "Dancing with your chap at a knees-up don't hurt either. It was glorious."

"Where was this knees-up?" I asked curiously. It had been an age since I'd danced, or at least, it felt like it.

"You wouldn't approve, Mrs. H. It were a gin house, but Caleb and I didn't take no gin. We was there for the piano and the fiddle, and we danced until we nearly dropped."

Taverns and gin houses often offered music and dancing to entice customers in to purchase spirits. Tess was correct that I did not approve of gin, which led too many to their ruin, but I could not admonish her for enjoying herself.

I was tempted, as we worked, to ask Tess to bid Caleb—Constable Greene of Scotland Yard—to tell me everything he could find out about the death of one Hiram Mobley of the Strand. However, when I'd turned to Caleb for assistance in the past, he'd nearly landed himself in a good deal of trouble, so I resisted. Inspector McGregor, his superior, had not taken kindly to me using the constable to gain information.

I hesitated to question Inspector McGregor as well, understanding why Lord Clifford wanted his own name kept out of this situation. My concern was more for Cynthia than her father, but I knew Inspector McGregor could fix upon a suspect and squeeze him until he was a pathetic pulp of a human being.

"Angel of mercy, indeed," I muttered.

"What's that, Mrs. H.?" Tess looked up at me.

"Nothing," I said. "I'm off to scatter largesse."

I took up my basket and a shawl and went up the outside stairs. It was my habit to distribute the food scraps to the hungry who would gather near the house at this hour, knowing of my generosity. The food would be thrown away if not eaten, so why let it go to waste?

I did not see James, Daniel's son, who sometimes lingered, both to make certain I was unharmed by those who swarmed to me or to offer his services as an errand runner. The fact that James was nowhere in sight did not mean he wasn't lurking. I sent the shadows a significant glance, hoping James, if there, would understand my silent message.

Whether James had been present or not, once the rest of the staff and Lord Clifford had gone to bed later that night, a quiet knock sounded on the back door. I opened it to find Daniel McAdam on the doorstep.

CHAPTER 3

These days when Daniel, a delivery man with thick dark hair and very blue eyes, visited at night, he greeted me with a soft but fiery kiss. He did so this night as well.

One day I'd succumb to him. Whether that surrender would be wise and beautiful or a very foolish action, I had not yet decided.

For now, I returned the kiss with warmth and led him into my kitchen.

I always held a dish back for Daniel in anticipation of his visits. Tonight, it was a portion of the bubble and squeak, which I'd topped with extra sausage. Daniel's eyes widened appreciatively when I slid the plate in front of him at the table.

"Lord Clifford is here," I said.

Daniel froze in the act of taking his first bite. He stared up at me then continued to masticate, his expression changing from consternation to blissful enjoyment.

He swallowed. "This is heaven, Kat."

I pretended not to warm to his praise as I sat down across from him. "It is nought but cabbage and potatoes. For peasants to eat after a long day in the fields."

"Lucky peasants, if *you* cooked it for them." Daniel's sincerity radiated. "Lord Clifford arrived, you say? That is interesting."

"It is a devilish nuisance, you mean. *And* he's gotten himself into a bit of bother, which is no amazing thing."

As Daniel continued eating—really, he must starve himself all the day long the way he shoveled it in—I related Lord Clifford's tale.

"I see he is as wily as ever," Daniel said when I'd finished. He scraped up the last of the gravy with his fork. "Though not as wily as he believes, from what you say. I agree that his friend Jacoby was about to fleece Lord Clifford as much as he'd intended to fleece Mr. Dougherty." He licked the fork clean.

"Great luck for Lord Clifford that the moneylender was killed." I rose to fetch the kettle I'd set on the stove and carried it to the table. "Which is what the police will say."

I poured a trickle of very hot water from the kettle into the teapot, letting the sound soothe me. I set the lid back on the teapot and returned the kettle to the stove.

"Plenty of people will benefit from Mobley the Moneylender being no more," Daniel said as I reseated myself. "Not only Lord Clifford."

"Which means anyone in London could have killed the man," I said, discouraged.

Daniel shook his head. "Not anyone. This murderer would have to get past the toughs Mobley surrounded himself with, or be someone Mobley would trust. If someone desperate rushed past the ruffians, the murderer might have been killed as well."

"And their body dropped into the Thames," I finished. "In that case, we might never know who killed Mobley."

"Unless the police interrogate said toughs. Though I imagine those Mobley employed have discreetly disappeared or at least found a new post."

"If it was someone Mobley trusted, it might have been a friend," I mused. "Or a brother or cousin. Or one of his own ruffians."

"It is certainly worth looking into. I haven't heard of Mobley, but I know men in the moneylending business. One of them might have some knowledge of what happened."

Mobley's rivals, Daniel meant. In the underworld, criminals kept themselves informed of one another's actions. One had to be careful not to intrude on the wrong patch.

"Then there is Mr. Jacoby." I lifted the teapot and refreshed our cups with the fragrant liquid. "He purportedly owns a shipping company. If Lord Clifford began to fuss about the money he now owed Mr. Mobley—and couldn't pay back—perhaps Mr. Jacoby solved the problem for him."

"A possibility," Daniel conceded.

I'd had a notebook already open on the table before Daniel arrived, but it was one in which I'd been making notes on my recipes. Its pages were stained with sauce and smears of butter, but it was more precious to me than the second-hand cookbooks I'd returned to the housekeeper's parlor.

My dear friend Joanna had given me a new notebook last Christmas, which I kept put away so it would not be dirtied. I now retrieved it from a drawer in the dresser, opening it to a blank page when I resumed my seat.

Mr. Mobley, I wrote across the top. "We need to find out more about Mobley. Was he married? Did he have children? I hope not, for the poor mites' sakes. Who were his brothers and sisters? Friends? People he especially trusted?"

"I'll go to the Strand in the morning, have a poke around," Daniel offered.

"I rather hoped you'd be able to look at the police findings on the death. They must have already begun an investigation."

"Mm." Daniel rested his elbows on the table and lifted his teacup in both hands. "Any curiosity I betray will reach certain ears. I will try to have a glance at their files, if I can, but I believe I'll learn more by going straight to Mobley's shop."

"By 'certain ears,' you mean Mr. Monaghan," I said darkly.

Daniel took a noisy sip of tea and set down his cup. "He is keeping me on a short tether these days." His voice was tight, betraying his frustration.

Monaghan was Daniel's guv'nor at Scotland Yard, a man who had no title I could discern, but whom the other inspectors and superintendents walked softly around. Daniel was in thrall to him for a past transgression that Monaghan had taken personally.

I wasn't certain which worried me more—Daniel investigating a moneylender and his criminal connections, or Mr. Monaghan sending Daniel into danger because Daniel had asked too many questions.

I let out a sigh. "I wish I did not worry about you so much."

Daniel had the audacity to grin. "I rather like you worrying. It means you might care for me a bit."

My face grew hot. I had not meant to admit such a truth.

"I do care, you daft man. Why else would I have kept back the bubble and squeak for you? The rest of the staff and Lord Clifford devoured most of it. I went to great effort to hide it from them."

"I see." Daniel gazed at me so long my face heated further.

"Well," I said briskly, trying to banish the troubling feelings inside me. "We have many tasks ahead of us. Where do we begin?"

————

I made my start in the morning by cooking breakfast for the ten staff in the house and Lord Clifford.

Before Daniel had departed, we'd made a possible list of suspects. I'd jotted these in my notebook, wishing to divide the lot between us for investigation. Daniel then said he'd take most of them, as it would be too dangerous for me to walk through London asking questions about a dead moneylender, which left me little to do.

At least, so Daniel supposed.

With the family away, I had a bit more freedom to come and go, even when it was not my day out, though I would not take too much advantage of that. I still had plenty of work to do, and I did not wish Mr. Davis or Mrs. Redfern to believe I was shirking my duties or deserting them.

Not that Mr. Davis didn't spend long hours in his butler's pantry reading newspapers, or that Mrs. Redfern didn't use the time to write letters to every member of her family and all her acquaintance. I saw no difference in me occupying myself by walking about London, as long as I was home when needed.

I invented the excuse of visiting Covent Garden market

to find the best comestibles for new dishes I wanted to attempt in the family's absence. Tess declared stoutly that she could make a start on luncheon without me, so I headed out after breakfast in coat and hat, a basket on my arm.

Covent Garden was a long way from my true destination, but I began to walk that direction as I left the house in Mount Street. When I reached Regent Street, I found an omnibus heading east and climbed aboard, clutching my basket on my lap as the crowded omnibus trundled along to the Strand.

I decided to leave the moneylender and his ruffians to Daniel but let my curiosity take me farther east, past the Tower of London. I abandoned the omnibus in Fleet Street and took the underground, a thing I disliked doing, but it saved much walking, to emerge near the soaring walls of the Tower.

Beyond the Tower, I entered the docklands. Warehouses and a large railroad depot lined the street on which I walked, interspersed with music halls and gin houses—entertainment for the dockworkers and sailors when they left their duties. These men worked very hard, and I did not begrudge them their brief time of pleasure, but I thought that pouring gin down their throats was not the wisest course. My own husband had been a sailor on merchant ships, and gin had done him no good at all.

Wellclose Square lay a little way beyond the Royal Mint. Daniel, who was rife with historical details about London, had told me that this square had been the home of ships' officers and well-heeled gentlefolk a few centuries ago. A church designed by the father of a famous actor and playwright, Colley Cibber, had stood at its center.

The expansion of the docklands had changed the face of

the square over the years. Now almshouses filled the streets in spaces that didn't have public houses and gin halls. The Sailors' Home—where working sailors could board while in port—ran half the length of Wells Street, which flanked the square, and a house for sailors who'd become too enfeebled to labor sat on the other end of it. I wondered if those who lived in the first ever believed they'd finish up in the second.

Mr. Jacoby's business sat halfway along the west side of the square. The sign over the door of the building, which looked no different to those surrounding it, proclaimed *Jacoby and Sons, Shippers.*

The door was unlocked, so I pushed my way inside. I found myself entering a narrow hallway with two doors on either side of it. One door held a thick lock but the other, which had the label *Office* tacked onto it, was ajar. I opened it and peered in.

"Good morning," I called.

I received no reply. The office was dim and dusty, with a hardwood floor that needed scrubbing. One desk reposed in a corner, with only a blotter and an ink stand on top of it. Two clerks' desks, which clerks would stand behind, faced the door, but no clerks were in sight.

I spied another door behind the large desk. I boldly marched to it, settled my basket firmly on my arm, and knocked.

I heard rustling and voices, mostly asking each other who the devil could be disturbing them. I retreated to the other side of the desk before a plump, middle-aged man yanked the door open. He stopped short when he saw me, as though expecting—or fearing—someone entirely different.

"Yes, madam?" he asked impatiently. "How can I help you?"

"This is a shipping company, is it not?" I inquired.

The man fixed me a look that said he did not approve of women charging into offices that were obviously the enclaves of men. "It is. What about it, madam?"

I put on a firm expression. "I would like to speak to Mr. Jacoby, please. I might have business for him."

The man's bushy brows climbed. He wasn't much taller than me, and his soft limbs and belly gave him a round shape. His receding sandy-colored hair contributed to this overall form as did the fact that he was clean shaven, though his eyebrows were thick.

"*I* am Mr. Jacoby. I very much doubt you have an appointment, Mrs.—"

"Davis." I said the first name that popped into my head and hoped Mr. Davis would forgive me. Not that I would ever let him find out I'd appropriated his name for my purposes. "If I wanted to ship a quantity of woolens, what would I—?"

I never found out whether Mr. Jacoby would view me as a potential client or throw me out, because at that moment, another man charged into the office behind me.

"Jacoby!" Lord Clifford shouted. "*Swindler.* I thought we were friends, you swine."

He hurtled around the desk and charged Mr. Jacoby, reaching out to close his hands around the other man's thick neck.

CHAPTER 4

I seized Lord Clifford by the arm and tried to haul him backward. I could not pull him fully away, but I was at least strong enough to prevent him from reaching Jacoby.

Jacoby retreated a step, but instead of rushing to safety, he adjusted his cravat and stared at Lord Clifford in amazement.

"Swindler? *Me?* Clifford, whatever do you mean?"

"Mrs. Holloway is right." Lord Clifford wrested himself from my hold, but he did not resume his attack on Jacoby. "You planned to dupe me out of as much money as you did Dougherty. I *trusted* you. Now a man is dead, and if his successors come after me for that debt … *You* should pay it. Why don't you hand me fifteen thousand guineas on the moment?"

Jacoby blinked at Lord Clifford in bewilderment, but I saw the canniness in his eyes as he tried to think of a way to turn this dilemma to his advantage.

"Who is Mrs. Holloway?" Jacoby asked. "She is obviously

a siren temptress trying to sway you into doubting me. Perhaps *she* wants the money."

Lord Clifford stared at Jacoby, baffled. "Mrs. Holloway is a cook. And she is standing right here." He indicated me.

In the very back of my mind, I took some offense that Lord Clifford could never view me—or any cook for that matter—as a siren temptress. Cooks could be temptresses as much as anyone else, once we put aside our unflattering work attire.

My more immediate reaction, however, was dismay that Lord Clifford had exposed my ruse. Mr. Jacoby pinned me with a steely gaze.

"She told me her name was Mrs. Davis."

"I misspoke," I said quickly. "Davis is my maiden name." Actually, it was Holloway, which I'd resumed after the death of my rather horrible husband, but Mr. Jacoby did not need to know my history.

Jacoby's eyes narrowed, but Lord Clifford waved the confusion away. "Whatever you call her, she pointed out that you were drawing me into this scheme alongside Dougherty. You coaxed me in by telling me how much I could make once we finished with him."

"Because my company will do very well, once I have it running smoothly," Jacoby answered, assurance oozing from him. "Dougherty's capital would have been enough to make us both rich."

"And *my* capital," Lord Clifford snapped. "I have a wife and daughter to look after. If I'm out that fifteen thousand I owed Mobley, my family will go to a workhouse. My darling daughter will have to hire herself out as a governess or some such awful thing. You owe me that money, Jacoby."

"Surely you can raise it, your lordship." Jacoby's smoothness of manner returned. "You are a peer of the realm."

"Shows you know nothing about the bloody aristocracy," Lord Clifford muttered.

Jacoby went on in the same unruffled tone. "You are trusting the word of an ignorant cook over mine? When I am an experienced investor?"

"She is *not* an ignorant cook. She is very clever. She helped me work a scheme with a necklace last year that exposed an anarchist. From what I understand, the police were most appreciative to find him."

I tried to make myself inconspicuous behind Lord Clifford and willed him to cease speaking. Jacoby turned his glare on me.

"Are you working a scheme on me now?" he demanded, more of me than Lord Clifford. "Will the police be here soon to haul me to a magistrate?" He peered past me as though a few helmeted constables would thunder in any moment.

"No," Lord Clifford said in confusion. "Why would I alert the confounded magistrates?" He poked a finger toward Jacoby's soft middle. "If Mobley's mates come after me for that fifteen thousand, and you do not supply it, I am finished with you. What's more, I will ruin you. That, at least, is something my title is good for."

Jacoby's ingratiating manner deserted him, and he regarded Lord Clifford coolly. Too coolly, as though he had no fear of Lord Clifford's influence. "Then you had better leave, your lordship. Or *I* will summon the police to remove you and your precious cook from my premises."

"*Ruin you.*" Lord Clifford jabbed his finger one more time in Jacoby's direction and then turned on his heel. "Come along, Mrs. Holloway. Let us shake the dust of this place from our feet."

I'd not had the chance to question Jacoby—I'd planned to ask whether he had been near the moneylender's shop on the day of Mobley's murder, and whether he knew the money-lender at all—but I had little choice except to follow Lord Clifford out.

I paused on the threshold to glance back at Jacoby. Whether I meant to apologize or say something polite so he wouldn't rush after me and clout me, as many felt they had the right to do to servants, I wasn't certain.

Jacoby wasn't looking at me. He watched Lord Clifford stride away, and the hardness on his face told me he would not soon dismiss the earl's threats. He was a dangerous man. Lord Clifford, I realized, did not understand how dangerous.

I turned and hurried out before Jacoby could notice me.

Once outside, I drew a breath of the sharp October air. Autumn had arrived in London, with gray clouds piling in the east and a stiff breeze flowing up the Thames.

I reached Lord Clifford as he passed the music hall, shut and quiet this early, and turned the corner into Cable Street. He was going the entirely wrong way if he intended to return to Mayfair, but he was marching in a fury, paying no attention to his surroundings.

"Perhaps we should find a hansom, your lordship," I panted as I trotted next to him.

"Eh?" Lord Clifford peered at me as though he'd forgotten my presence. "Oh, I suppose." He waved at one that was racing along the street, its horse's legs a blur. The driver utterly ignored us. "Damn and blast the fellow."

I tugged his sleeve. "There is a stand at the next corner. We have to queue."

"I haven't queued for anything since I was a young man scratching for a living," Lord Clifford growled, but he let me lead him toward Prince's Square. "Do you know, Mrs. Holloway, that being related to an earl means you can still be dirt poor? And said earl doesn't give a damn? Not that the peerage endowed me with any large sums once I inherited it. Probably my cousin, the former earl, didn't have two coins to rub together, either. It's a funny old world, isn't it?"

His rage at Jacoby seemed to have dissipated. Lord Clifford regarded me with sadness, his eyes red-rimmed, as though he'd shed a few tears since racing from Jacoby's office.

At the turning to Prince's Square, I hailed one of the hansoms that slowed, seeking new fares. I bundled Lord Clifford inside the cab and gave the driver our direction in Mount Street.

The cabby barely let me sit down before the vehicle jerked forward. I clutched my basket securely and balanced on the seat.

Lord Clifford gazed into the street as we passed delivery wagons and people moving about in their daily labors. His entire body drooped. "I've been a complete fool, haven't I? I thought I was so clever, believed Jacoby a trustworthy mate."

"Have you known Mr. Jacoby long?" I asked.

Lord Clifford shrugged. "For years, though I haven't seen him since I became a respectable aristocrat. Jacoby was always good for a scheme, and I usually came out of it well. He has changed," he concluded sorrowfully.

"As have you, your lordship. Perhaps now that you are a peer, Mr. Jacoby regards you more as a mark than an ally."

"That is it exactly. How on earth am I to tell my poor wife that I might have lost us fifteen thousand guineas? We do not have it. As my daughter is always quick to point out, the Shires family is skint."

"Perhaps you will not owe the money." I tried to sound hopeful. "Mr. Mobley was a villain, was he not? The police might close down his business entirely, in which case you'd not be beholden to anyone trying to collect the debt."

"The police." Lord Clifford snorted. "My dear, I have had my fill of the police for my lifetime. When they came to investigate my beloved son's death, do you know what the detective inspector told me?" He faced me, his expression one of rage combined with bleak sorrow. "That *I* was to blame for poor Reggie shooting himself. That I should have known he was in a bad way and ought to have locked up all the guns. And do you know, Mrs. Holloway?" Lord Clifford's eyes filled with tears that drove away the anger and left only grief. "The inspector was right. I know that, if not for me, my Reggie would still be alive and with us."

Lord Clifford put his gloved hand over his eyes and bowed his head.

CHAPTER 5

I beheld Lord Clifford in silent compassion as the cab sped its way around the Tower to the Minories. His shoulders quivered, but I let him cry without embarrassing him with exclamations of sympathy.

I doubted very much that Lord Clifford had been to blame for his son's death, and I grew angry at the unnamed inspector for telling him so. What a cruel thing to say to a man who'd just lost his son.

From what little Lady Cynthia had related to me about her brother, I'd gleaned that the Honorable Reginald Shires had been a wild young man, prone to deep play, amassing large debts he couldn't pay. He'd also been one for the ladies —those with expensive tastes—which hadn't helped. He'd been in despair the night he'd died, Cynthia had told me, though about what, she hadn't known. He'd been quite inebriated on top of this, a bad combination.

However, I knew the death of a loved one could bring much guilt, whether that loved one had passed peacefully from a lingering illness or abruptly in a shocking way.

If only we'd realized what was happening, we would think. If only we had worked harder to prevent it, hadn't been paying attention to our own lives, had been there more for them.

It had been several years after my mother's death before I realized that, unless I'd suddenly acquired divine powers, I could not have forestalled her passing. She'd urged me to take the position in a good kitchen as under-cook, which would be excellent training for me, and wouldn't hear of me staying home to take care of her.

She'd known even then that she was ill, I'd understood long afterward. She'd been making certain I could make a living on my own once she was gone.

Even now, more than a decade on, these thoughts made my eyes sting.

I believed Lord Clifford had no reason to feel such guilt, but he'd been the lad's father—an ineffectual father, from what Cynthia said. He could not help but feel responsible.

Also, young Reginald had been Lord Clifford's heir, and gentlemen set much store by their heirs. Male ones, that was. Daughters were inconvenient beings that had to be married off, and it was rather scandalous when they were not. Lord Clifford had managed to see one daughter married— Cynthia's sister, Emily—and then he'd lost her as well.

The cab left Aldgate Street for Fenchurch Street and meandered through the City to Cheapside, where people lingered to watch Mr. John Bennett's entertaining clock chime the hour. As we passed Clover Lane, which opened from Cheapside, I gazed longingly into the narrow passage-way. Near the end of it was the small house where my friend Joanna kept my daughter safe.

I hugged my basket and shrank into the corner of the

hansom as Clover Lane fell behind us. If anything happened to Grace, I would be devastated. While I was a cook and Lord Clifford a lofty earl, we shared that understanding.

When the hansom trundled past Temple Bar and rattled into the Strand, Lord Clifford suddenly came alert.

"Driver," he shouted. "Stop here."

The cabby abruptly pulled the horse past two wagons and halted at the side of the road. Lord Clifford slammed open the folding door of the hansom and leapt to the pavement.

I scrambled out after him, certain I knew what he intended. Above me, the cabby snarled invective—he hadn't been paid.

"Wait there, please," I called up to him, and hurried through the crowd after Lord Clifford.

I barely kept the earl's thin back in sight but caught up to him when he turned to a door and plunged through it. The door was not marked, but I knew in my bones that it led to the establishment of one Hiram Mobley, moneylender.

"Your lordship, I do not think this is a good idea—"

I tried to grasp his coat, but Lord Clifford evaded me. He charged down a hall similar to the one that had led to Mr. Jacoby's office and pounded on the door at the end.

"Open up," he bellowed. "I've come to tell you you'll get nothing from me, do you understand? I'll have the law—"

The door was wrenched open, but no moneylender or his ruffians appeared on the threshold. Instead, Lord Clifford gaped at a tall, slim-faced man of about thirty in a neat black suit. The man's pale hair was combed and pomaded back from his sharp face, and a pair of light blue eyes skewered Lord Clifford without fear.

I stepped into the shadows, knowing full well what sort of gent this was, and I had no wish for him to notice me. I saw no sign of Daniel anywhere—if he'd been investigating in Mobley's office, as he'd said he intended to, he'd have come forward to assist.

"You'll have the law do what, sir?" the tall man inquired in a cool tone.

"Arrest the lot of you," Lord Clifford spluttered. "You're extortionists and thieves, and I owe you nothing."

The man did not change expression. "If there is any arresting, sir, I will be the one doing it. I am Detective Sergeant Scott, looking into the murder of Mr. Hiram Mobley. Who might you be?"

Lord Clifford drew back. "Oh. Well. Good. So you should."

"You did not answer my question, sir." Sergeant Scott spoke with calm assurance.

"No? I am the Earl of Clifford, young man. I'll leave you to it, shall I?" He attempted a negligent gesture. "You carry on."

Scott gave him a shallow bow that held no deference. "Your lordship. Mind if I ask you a question or two, now that you're here?"

Lord Clifford stiffened. "Why the devil should you?"

I could have told Lord Clifford that this was exactly the wrong thing to say. Arrogantly swearing to a detective from Scotland Yard would only convince him of one's guilt.

"I meant to pay a call on you, your lordship," the sergeant said. "You're on a list of gentlemen who owed Mr. Mobley a powerful lot of money. In addition, you came here on the afternoon of his murder and argued with him. The next morning, he was found dead. The doctor who examined him said he was killed sometime between ten o'clock that evening and midnight. Will you please tell me what happened? In your own words?"

Lord Clifford swung to me, his face holding stark fear, but I nodded at him encouragingly. The sergeant completely ignored me.

"I argued with him, because he was a swindler." Lord Clifford regained some of his composure. "He demanded I give him half again what I owed him, right away, if you please. Bloody cheek of the man. I refused, and he threatened me—and my family. I told him what I thought of him. Then I left. He was alive when I went out, Sergeant. Now, I have matters to attend to. Good day to you."

"Another moment, sir." Sergeant Scott's quiet voice was powerful enough to stop Lord Clifford from rushing out. Had I been here on my own, I'd have already been in the wind, but I wanted to make certain Cynthia's father returned safely home.

Lord Clifford turned back ungraciously. "What is it, now?"

"I'd like you accompany me to Scotland Yard, your lordship. To have a chat with my inspector and get your statement written out all proper."

"I will not," Lord Clifford stated in a haughty tone. "I told you, Sergeant, I am quite busy. Good day to you."

Any other police detective might be intimidated by angering an aristo, but Sergeant Scott was obviously not easily daunted.

"Constables," he barked. Two uniformed constables appeared, one from inside the office and another from the door behind me. "Lord Clifford, I am placing you under arrest for the murder of Mr. Hiram Mobley. As you are a peer, you'll not be locked in the cells, but you'll speak to my inspector, who'll then determine where and when you'll be examined."

"The devil I will." Lord Clifford glared at the sergeant for a moment, his back straight, then he did a foolish thing. He turned and sprinted for the outside world and freedom.

Lord Clifford barreled past me, and I scarcely avoided being slammed into a wall. He tried to charge past the constable in his way, but that constable was a beefy young man, who spread his arms to form an unmoving barrier.

Lord Clifford's fists came up, as though he planned to punch his way out. Perhaps such tactics had worked when he'd been a young man, fleecing others up and down the streets of London. He was middle-aged now and likely not as fit as he had been.

The muscular constable caught the blow Lord Clifford threw at him and pushed the earl backward.

"None of that, your lordship," Sergeant Scott said quietly. The second constable locked a cuff around Lord Clifford's wrist and the two young men hauled Lord Clifford out.

I stepped bravely in front of the sergeant, swallowing when he turned his sharp gaze on me. "Please, do not do this," I said shakily. "There is no need. Lord Clifford is distraught, but he's done nothing."

Sergeant Scott regarded me without benevolence. "Take yourself out of the way, missus, if you don't want to be nicked alongside him."

As worried about Lord Clifford as I was, I did as Sergeant Scott bade me. I reasoned, through the panic that started to grip me, that it would do no good for me to get myself banged up.

I'd seen the inside of a prison before, and I never wanted to see it again. If the sergeant arrested me, I'd be thrown into a dank cell while Lord Clifford was served tea in a detective inspector's office. I was nobody important.

"He is an earl," I tried.

"As I said, my inspector will sort it out." The sergeant set a low-crowned hat on his head. "Out you go."

He clearly did not know who I was or why I'd come with Lord Clifford, but he wasn't interested enough to discover anything more. He herded me out ahead of him into wind that had turned cold, then locked the front door firmly with an iron key.

I could only watch as Lord Clifford was bundled into a plain black carriage by the two constables, he struggling and protesting all the way. Sergeant Scott climbed in behind him and his men without a word, slamming the door. The driver gave a command to the horse and the carriage surged into traffic, leaving me alone.

I frantically scanned the street, as though Daniel would pop up out of nowhere and assist—to be fair, he sometimes did—but I saw nothing of him.

My panic, which memories of Newgate had engendered, faded. I made certain the carriage was long out of sight before I turned and headed back into the office that had once housed Mr. Mobley.

———

When I emerged from the offices again, I saw, to my amazement, that the cabbie had waited for me. Not out of concern or politeness, I understood. He didn't want to be out his fare, which now I'd be expected to pay.

"Regent Street, please," I said as I climbed inside.

This time, the man let me be seated before he charged away down the Strand.

I'd found nothing of interest in Mobley's office. Though the sergeant had locked the door—I assume Scotland Yard had taken charge of the keys when they'd carried away Mobley's dead body—I knew how to not let a lock stop me. A few hairpins sacrificed, and I was in.

The police must have removed anything suspicious, because I found mostly empty drawers. No ledgers, no stacks of cash or bags of coins, no strongboxes. No convenient letters from clients threatening to kill Mr. Mobley if they weren't given more time to pay back their loan, outlining the exact day and time they'd do it.

Nothing to point to anyone, including Lord Clifford, that I could see. Sergeant Scott must be a thorough young man.

I had not heard of Sergeant Scott, so I had no idea who his inspector was—not McGregor, whose subordinates I'd met. I would have to find out more about him.

At Regent Street, I paid the cabbie more shillings than I truly wanted to part with but also gave him my thanks for staying with me. He drove away with a brief nod and didn't look back.

I entered the tall house that was my destination, hefted my basket, and made my way upstairs to a higher floor. I did not see the landlady on my way, so I could not inquire whether the gentleman I sought was at home. He might or might not be at the Polytechnic, where he'd become ardently absorbed in his work, but I had to try. If he wasn't here, I'd make my way to Cavendish Square and hope to be admitted to his office.

I tapped on the door at the top of the long flight and was rewarded with a thin voice saying, "Enter."

A slender young man with very dark hair and a pair of spectacles hunched over a desk against a wall, absorbed in the three books and several sheets of paper spread before him. He did not look up when I walked inside and closed the door, as though he'd forgotten anyone had knocked.

"Mr. Thanos?" I ventured.

His head jerked up. Mr. Thanos swung around in his chair, blinked a moment, and then hurtled to his feet.

"Mrs. Holloway." He bounded across the carpet to me, beaming a wide smile. "What a delight. Sit down, sit down. I'll have my landlady bring us up some tea and as many cakes as you wish."

When Mr. Thanos expressed delight to see a person, he meant it. Any other man might simply attempt politeness, hiding his annoyance that I'd interrupted him, but Mr. Thanos was quite sincere.

"No need." I held up my hands to keep him from rushing out to the staircase and calling for the tea. "I must leave at once. I have come to ask if you could find Daniel—Mr. McAdam—for me."

Mr. Thanos's dark eyes widened behind the thick glass of his spectacles. "What makes you believe I can find McAdam any quicker than you can? The man is as elusive as a ghost. And ghosts do not exist, as you know."

I shook my head. "What I mean is, I need help finding him. I would rush about London seeking him myself, but it is not my day out, and I cannot stay away from home much longer."

As my desperation reached him. Mr. Thanos softened with sympathy. "Of course, my dear Mrs. Holloway, I will be most happy to assist. You seem unhappy. Is something amiss?" His concern, like his joy at my visit, was true.

"Cynthia's father has been arrested." Before Mr. Thanos could splutter questions, I rushed on. "I need Daniel to find out what is happening and make certain Lord Clifford is released. At once. He no more killed the moneylender in the Strand than I did."

"Good heavens." Mr. Thanos stared. "Are you speaking of *that* murder? It was in the newspapers. Why the devil should anyone believe Lord Clifford had anything to do with it? He's a congenial chap. I've had fine chats with him."

"You read the newspapers?" I asked. This was the most astonishing statement in Mr. Thanos's last speech. He rarely lifted his nose from thick tomes on calculus, electromagnetism, and other mysterious topics.

"My landlady peruses them all." Mr. Thanos waved fingers stained with ink. "She especially loves sordid crimes—as long as they happen far from her. She told me of it. But why—?"

"I will explain everything in time, Mr. Thanos," I assured him. "I must hurry off. Please, if you find Daniel, send him to Scotland Yard at once. Or send word if you are unsuccessful. I have other means of prying him out if necessary."

"Of course, of course. I will go immediately." Mr. Thanos snatched a coat from the stand beside the door and began to put it on wrong-side out.

I slid it from him, turned the sleeves the right way around, and helped settle it on his shoulders. He thanked me profusely, grabbed his hat, and opened the door for me, ushering me out ahead of him.

We went down the stairs together. Mr. Thanos offered to find—and pay for—a hansom to take me home, but I declined. It wasn't far, and I'd run to Mount Street faster than a horse and cab could wind through the heavy traffic.

I thanked him, letting Mr. Thanos wring my hand. He'd come out without gloves but still wearing his spectacles, which he disliked being seen in. Before I could mention either, he spun from me and dashed up the street, waving at hansoms who rushed past him.

I turned my steps for Mount Street. I was right that I could reach the house quickly, and soon I was clattering down its outside stairs to the kitchen. My basket was still empty of comestibles, but that couldn't be helped.

Tess looked up from where she chopped onions, her eyes streaming from their pungent emissions.

"Oh, Mrs. H., I'm that glad you're home. Lady Cynthia's here. She's upstairs in her chamber, but very upset, Mrs. Redfern says. She wants to see you, and was that unhappy when Mrs. Redfern told her you were out. You'd better—"

Before Tess could finish telling me what I needed to do, the backstairs door banged, and a harried tread sounded in the flagstone hall.

A moment later, Lady Cynthia, dressed in well-tailored trousers and man's coat, strode with her usual vigor into the kitchen.

"*There* you are, Mrs. H.," she proclaimed. "I was about to tramp the streets searching for you. Mummy told me my errant father escaped his tethers and came to Town. We haven't heard a blasted word from the man since. Mrs. Redfern says he arrived *here,* but he's gone off again. Do you know what the devil has become of him?"

CHAPTER 6

ess watched me with rounded eyes that were red from the onions, Cynthia in worried impatience. I set my empty basket on the dresser and contemplated how best to answer Lady Cynthia's question.

"Perhaps we should go into the housekeeper's parlor," I suggested to Cynthia.

Her annoyed concern turned to alarm. "Please tell me now, Mrs. Holloway. What has happened? Is my father dead?"

"What?" I started. "No, indeed, he was alive and well when last I saw him."

Cynthia exhaled in relief, but her urgency didn't ebb. "*Tell me, Mrs. H. I don't mind if Tess hears. She already knows much about my benighted family.*"

I glanced to see who else was nearby. The footmen not upstairs under Mr. Davis's thumb were being loud and merry in the servants' hall. Elsie washed up in the scullery, singing at the top of her voice. The boot boy, Charlie, should be upstairs in his bunk, taking a nap or studying his reading.

I gave him very light duties when the family was not in residence.

When I was satisfied I wouldn't be overheard, I leaned to Cynthia. "Lord Clifford has been arrested. I am so sorry. I could not stop it."

Cynthia groaned and dramatically slapped her forehead. "What has he done this time? Break it to me gently. Who has he bamboozled? The Prime Minister? A royal prince?"

"I am afraid the police believe he committed murder."

Cynthia's hand came down, and she stared at me in amazement. Her eyes were very light blue, a different color from but the same shape as her father's.

"Murder? Papa? Absolute rot. The man can't bear to squash a bug." Cynthia gazed at me as though willing me to tell her it had all been a mistake. I was certain it had been, but I had no answers. "Where is he? Bow Street?"

"I believe he was taken straight to the Yard," I said. "I am trying to find out what will happen to him."

Cynthia grew suddenly solicitous. "My dear, Mrs. H., I have no doubt you did everything you could. My father in trouble is a common thing, I'm sorry to say, though it's not usually this bad. I'll go to Scotland Yard at once and speak to that inspector fellow—McGregor. He doesn't like me, but he's a reasonable chap."

"It might not be that simple. It is not his case." I explained about Sergeant Scott and how he'd indicated he'd have Lord Clifford speak to his inspector, though not that inspector's name. "McGregor might be able to do nothing."

"Doesn't hurt to try. I'm off then. Come with me, Mrs. H.?"

I hesitated. "I have Mr. Thanos looking for Daniel, and I

will bid James to as well if I can find him. Daniel will be able to secure Lord Clifford's release, I'm certain of it."

"McAdam can work wonders," Cynthia agreed. "But I'm not the sort who's willing to sit and wait."

Neither was I, but I was much more restricted than Cynthia, a fact she did not always remember.

"Go on, Mrs. H.," Tess urged. "It's only the staff to get meals for, and I can do that. They know I won't take none of their lip if they don't like what I cook."

I preferred them to enjoy their meals, but I was grateful for Tess's help. "Mr. Davis will be most annoyed," I said, prevaricating.

"We'll make it up to him," Tess assured me. "You need to go spring his lordship."

"Thank you, Tess. I'll make it up to *you* as well." I observed Cynthia's attire. "Perhaps you should change into something more conventional," I said as tactfully as I could.

Cynthia gazed down at herself. "You mean they might arrest me if I go barging into Scotland Yard in my frock coat and trousers? Ah, well, you are likely right. I'll rush upstairs and change into a frock so I can bat my eyelashes and all that rot. Pretend to be a shrinking female distraught about her papa." She hesitated, worry entering her voice again. "They can't truly believe my father had anything to do with a murder, can they?"

I nodded with reluctance. "Lord Clifford was heard arguing with the man, and he's being very vague on what exactly happened."

Cynthia heaved a long sigh. "Dear Papa is not the wisest of persons when it comes to the law. He learned in his early days that the less one says to the police, the better. Be back in a tick."

She rushed out with her usual verve, and soon we heard her ascending the stairs.

"How awful," Tess said as she resumed her onion chopping. "Want me to ask Caleb to have a listen and find out what's happening?"

"No," I said quickly. "I do not want to land the lad in more trouble."

"He's learned to be marvelously discreet. Besides, last time his prying did help Inspector McGregor catch a killer."

"Be that as it may, I would like Constable Greene to remain employed." I put away my empty basket and tried to gather ingredients for supper but only wandered ineffectually from dresser to table. "He likes being a policeman."

"He does that. Wants to make sergeant someday. And become a detective. Then I can help him on *his* cases." Tess brightened as she wove dreams of her future.

"I will see what I can find out with Lady Cynthia. If Daniel turns up here, please tell him where I've gone. We will hold Caleb in reserve."

"Right you are."

Tess's knife clacked happily against the board. I knew that if Caleb walked past on his beat, Tess would tell him everything, but that couldn't be helped. Constable Greene was turning out to be a wise lad, though too kindhearted for the police, in my opinion.

I gave up trying to focus on cooking and shrugged on my coat again when I heard Cynthia return.

She'd donned a light gray walking gown trimmed with dark violet piping, topping that with a matching jacket and a hat with drooping feathers.

In such an ensemble, she ought to be leaving by the front door to step into her carriage. Instead, she swept out through the scullery, making Elsie jump. Water nearly splashed Cynthia's fine skirts, missing them by a fraction of an inch.

I made a reassuring gesture at the startled Elsie and followed Cynthia up the stairs, struggling to keep up with her brisk pace.

We found a hansom in Berkeley Square. While Lord Clifford had indicated he'd brought his carriage and coachman to London, they were not in Mount Street, and I had no idea where he'd put them up. The Bywaters had given their own coachman a holiday—why pay the man to idle in his rooms above the stables while they were gone? Lesser paid grooms could take care of the horses.

Cynthia directed the driver to Scotland Yard. As we rode, I explained the whole affair to Cynthia—her father's involvement with Mr. Jacoby and Mr. Dougherty, what he'd borrowed from Mr. Mobley, and why. I'd not wished to distress her with the tale, but now I could not justify keeping it from her. Cynthia listened in dismay but not much surprise.

The roads were clogged with traffic, and after a considerable time, we descended in the narrow lane that opened just south of Charing Cross and entered the building that housed the Metropolitan Police.

I had been in this noisy hallway with its counter, desks, and milling constables too many times—once, I'd needed to access the morgue and discover whether Daniel had been killed. I tried to forget that awful day as we walked inside.

A woman huddled on a bench in a corner, keeping her two children close. I wondered if she'd come to find out what had happened to a husband, son, sister, mother, or to report a crime that had devastated her. I sent her my compassion.

Cynthia stepped up to the counter and rapped upon it. "I am here to see whatever inspector arrested the Earl of Clifford," she announced.

The sergeant in charge gazed at Cynthia sharply and without respect, I am sad to relate. I'd encountered this man before and knew he hadn't much use for women, even aristocratic ones.

"Sergeant Scott brought him in," I supplied. "There has been a misunderstanding."

The desk sergeant recognized me, but his sneer didn't lessen. "You ladies need to go home and wait for word. You can't be swanning in demanding to speak to inspectors."

Lady Cynthia became her most imperious self. "Now, see here—"

"It's all right, sergeant." Daniel's welcome rumble floated over us. "I'll take them up."

"McAdam," the sergeant growled as Daniel stepped off the stairs and approached. He obviously didn't like Daniel interrupting his remonstrations to forward women.

Daniel gestured for us to follow. "I agree with him in one respect," he said in a low voice as we joined him. "This is no place for you, Lady Cynthia. Or you, Kat."

"Nonsense," Cynthia scoffed. "My father never killed anyone. I'm here to take him home."

Daniel had long ago learned the futility of arguing with either of us. He led us up the stairs to the second floor without further word.

We trudged down a series of corridors in the long building to a thick wooden door set in the middle of one of the halls. Daniel tapped on it, and it was opened, to my surprise, by Mr. Thanos.

"Lady Cynthia," he exclaimed. Mr. Thanos's eyes, now

free of spectacles, fixed on her. I doubt he even noticed me standing behind her.

"Thanos found me and told me your tale," Daniel said. "Lord Clifford is speaking to Chief Inspector Ferguson at the moment."

Daniel tried to usher Cynthia and me into a busy outer office. Mr. Thanos, who'd remained standing in the doorway gazing at Cynthia, flushed and stepped back for us.

Sergeant Scott looked up in cold disdain from behind a desk but did not greet us. The other desks were taken up with various constables and clerks who busily sorted through papers, made notes in books, or carried sheafs to and fro. One young man in plain clothes was struggling to type on a typing machine with his two forefingers, one letter at a time.

The far wall held another door, closed, with the label *Chief Inspector Ferguson* painted on it.

"I offered to be a character witness for Lord Clifford," Daniel said. "I must inform you, Lady Cynthia, that your father is being too evasive about where he was the night Mobley was killed."

"Bloody hell," Cynthia stated loudly. Several of the constables glanced up in surprise at her language, but a few of them grinned at her. "Let me in there. I will make him tell me."

"Perhaps that might not be the wisest course," I suggested. If Lord Clifford was hiding his whereabouts, he might have been doing something *else* that could have him arrested.

"He is my father, Mrs. H., but he is a fool, and I need to extricate him from his follies. Take me in, McAdam."

Daniel, resigned, knocked softly on the inspector's door. A barked "Enter" had him opening it.

I caught a brief glimpse of Lord Clifford, his cravat awry, shoulders hunched as he sat on one side of a desk. On the other was a slender man with graying hair and a long nose, presumably Chief Inspector Ferguson. He had dark blue eyes that pinned us with a hard stare.

"Lord Clifford's daughter has arrived, sir," Daniel said deferentially.

Ferguson switched the stare to Cynthia alone, silently dismissing Mr. Thanos and me. Lord Clifford, who'd drawn a sharp breath when he'd seen Cynthia, shrank farther into his chair.

Ferguson nodded at Daniel, who gestured Cynthia in, but when Mr. Thanos and I tried to follow, Daniel stopped us. "Please wait," he said, sotto voce. "I'm sorry, Kat."

He closed the door, shutting the pair of us out.

"Well," Mr. Thanos huffed. "There's gratitude. After I raced all the way to Southampton Street in pursuit of him." He made a thin laugh, as though he joked, but I could see he was put out.

"Did you find him in Southampton Street?" Daniel had several hideaways around London. He flitted about the metropolis either in his job as deliveryman or investigating whatever he was sent to.

"No, I caught sight of McAdam striding along the Strand," Mr. Thanos explained. "I leapt out of the hansom, much to the cabbie's annoyance, and nearly tackled him. Once I told him of Lord Clifford's arrest, McAdam commandeered my cab, and we came here."

"I am pleased you did."

Mr. Thanos glowed under my praise, while I chafed to know what was being said inside the room. Short of bursting in, I would be in the dark until Daniel or Lady Cynthia could confer with me afterward.

A voice at my elbow made me jump. "What is McAdam's interest in this case?" Sergeant Scott had approached so quietly that neither of us had heard him. "Who exactly are *you*?" Scott demanded of me.

Mr. Thanos answered indignantly before I could speak. "She is Mrs. Holloway. Quite a respectable woman and also a jolly fine cook."

"A cook?" Scott gazed at me up and down as he would some sort of strange insect. "Lord Clifford's cook?"

"No, no, Lady Cynthia's," Mr. Thanos again answered for me. "Her family's that is. Lord Clifford is merely visiting."

"Why is the family cook being a minder to Lord Clifford?" Scott demanded, eyes still on me. "Why aren't you home fixing his steak and kidney pud?"

I drew myself up. "I do not like your tone, Sergeant." Cooks were among the senior staff of households, and I did not believe myself to be lower in status than a police sergeant. Also, I was a child of backstreet London. While we'd had proper fear of the police—who could arrest us for any imagined transgression—we'd also learned never to let on that they intimidated us. "Lord Clifford did have dealings with Mr. Mobley, but if there is no evidence he was near the man on the night in question, I believe you must let him go."

The sergeant definitely did not like a cook telling him how to do his job any more than I wanted him telling me mine. I sympathized with Sergeant Scott, as catching an elusive murderer when he had little to go on must be frustrating. Also, his inspector had shut him out of that room as neatly as he had us.

"Now you are his lordship's solicitor?" Scott asked me. "What was he doing at Mobley's establishment?"

"Looking for clues as to who killed Mr. Mobley," I said. "How exactly *was* he killed?"

"That is the police's business," Scott answered in irritation.

"It is also Lord Clifford's business," Mr. Thanos broke in. "As he has been accused of the crime."

"Lord Clifford's, yes." Scott acknowledged this with a hard nod. "Not yours."

While I longed for all the details, I understood his point. If he told us every aspect of the crime, we, as loyal friends to Lord Clifford, could concoct him an alibi.

Scott gestured toward the outer door. "Best you wait in the corridor. The inspector will not keep her ladyship long."

"And hopefully he will not keep his lordship, either," I said.

Scott had had enough of us. "Mrs. Holloway." He pointed to the door. "Mr.— er ..."

"Thanos," Mr. Thanos supplied cheerfully. "We will depart, do not worry. But if Lady Cynthia and Lord Clifford are here longer than they should be we *will* return with solicitors. Good afternoon."

Mr. Thanos offered me his arm and escorted me to the door. I noted the constables taking surreptitious glances at us as we passed. It was unlikely they'd ever witnessed ordinary folk twitting their severe sergeant.

Mr. Thanos and I exited into the hall. There were no seats about, as this was a thoroughfare and not a lounge, but I hovered, not minding standing. Or in my case, pacing.

The plainclothes constable who'd been painstakingly

typing slipped out a few minutes after our departure and quickly closed the door behind him. "Sir? Madam?"

Voice quiet, he indicated that we should follow him along the corridor to another small office. This one was dim, lit only by one narrow window. It was apparently unused, if the mismatched and much-scarred desks pushed against the walls were any indication. Storage for superfluous items, I guessed.

"I am Detective Constable Wallace," the young man addressed us. He had a freckled face and dark red hair, his eyes a deep brown. "I am working on the Mobley case, though my sergeant likes me to keep out of the way. But I am very certain the murderer was not the Earl of Clifford." He paused, glancing behind him as though fearing one of Sergeant Scott's toadies would follow to report on him. "If I have his lordship released, would he be willing to tell me all he knows?"

CHAPTER 7

While I debated how to answer Constable Wallace, Mr. Thanos spoke. "Only if you guarantee Lord Clifford can come home with us."

I was grateful to Mr. Thanos for grasping the essentials. "He might speak to you," I put in, trying to decide whether the young man was trustworthy. Constable Wallace seemed it, with his quiet confidence and steady gaze. He'd welcome our help, that gaze said, but he'd continue on his own course of action with or without it.

"I will arrange things," Wallace said. "The chief inspector can only recommend that Lord Clifford remains in London, preferably at home, until a hearing, and that is only if the inspector believes him guilty. Leave it with me."

"Thank you," Mr. Thanos said fervently. "You are a good man."

That remained to be seen. Wallace was ambitious, I saw, perhaps wishing to solve this case before the sergeant and catch the attention of Chief Inspector Ferguson. But if Wallace succeeded in having Lord Clifford released and proved he killed no one, I would not quibble about who the constable displaced as he moved up the ranks. If Sergeant Scott was competent, he'd deal with the lad or else learn to use his talents.

"Out of curiosity, who do you believe killed Mr. Mobley?" I asked Wallace.

The constable fixed me with cool assessment worthy of Inspector McGregor, then shrugged.

"His partner, most like. Man called Parkin. With Mobley gone, he takes over the business and any moneys Mobley might have had locked away. Placing Parkin at the scene is proving difficult, though. I'd like to hear what Lord Clifford has to say about his last visit to Mobley, and what else he observed, if anything."

My indignation rose. "If Mobley had a partner who inherited everything, why is Sergeant Scott not interrogating *him*? A much more likely candidate to be a murderer than poor Lord Clifford."

"The sergeant and the chief inspector have their eyes on him," Wallace assured me. "Sergeant Scott is thorough, if slow and careful. Me, I'd rather have Parkin sitting before me, and not let him out of the building until we are certain he did nothing. Parkin apparently is in Manchester, and was at the time of the murder, but that has yet to be determined. The police in Manchester have no reports to confirm him there."

"I am certain Lord Clifford will be happy to speak to you," I repeated. "Once he's at home." I would make sure he didn't flee back to Hertfordshire before Constable Wallace could turn up.

Constable Wallace gave me an understanding nod. "Wait here. I'll bring him out soon."

He departed, leaving Mr. Thanos and me alone in the dim and somewhat dispirited room. I'd speculated, when we entered, that unwanted things were stored here. At the moment, those unwanted things were myself and Mr. Thanos.

Mr. Thanos slid out a chair that was the least battered of the discarded lot, and gallantly gestured for me to sit. I did, as my feet were tired, and who knew how long we'd be kept waiting?

It was about twenty minutes, in fact. We heard voices in the corridor and emerged to see Chief Inspector Ferguson himself usher Lord Clifford, Lady Cynthia, and Daniel out of the main office. Constable Wallace and Sergeant Scott were nowhere in sight.

Lord Clifford's face was gray and haggard, but he walked with his head erect, his eyes filled with defiance. Cynthia had hold of his arm, and Daniel stuck close to his other side, as though to prevent him running off.

The chief inspector nodded at Mr. Thanos but ignored me. "As I said, please remain in Town for a few days, your lordship. Until everything is cleared up."

"He will," Lady Cynthia assured him in a firm voice.

"I will think on it," Lord Clifford said loftily. "It is my business if I return to Ardeley Hall. Everyone knows where it is."

He referred to his estate in Hertfordshire, near St. Albans. Lovely countryside, I had been told. I'd never been there myself.

"All the same," Ferguson said wearily.

"We will stay in London a while longer," Cynthia told the inspector. "There's no need to worry my mother about all this, is there, Papa?"

Lord Clifford winced. "Quite," he whispered.

Chief Inspector Ferguson gave Lord Clifford a polite bow. Lord Clifford nodded and strode away with Cynthia, his nose in the air. Rather overdoing his haughty earl act, I thought.

Daniel lingered to murmur something to Ferguson I did not catch. Then Daniel joined us, taking my arm to walk me out. Thanos bade Ferguson farewell before he fell into step beside Daniel and me.

A glance behind me showed Chief Inspector Ferguson standing by the door to his office, watching us. His expression was neutral, so I could not tell if he were angry, resigned, or satisfied that we were taking Lord Clifford away.

"How did you convince Chief Inspector Ferguson to let Lord Clifford go?" I burst out to Daniel as soon as we were in the street. Lady Cynthia and her father moved swiftly ahead of us as we turned the corner from Great Scotland Yard and on into Charing Cross. I wasn't certain whether Cynthia was searching for a hansom or intended to walk all the way home.

"He always meant to release him," Daniel answered. "Sergeant Scott brought in Lord Clifford in case he'd actually committed the crime, but Ferguson is no fool. He'll check Lord Clifford's weak story, but I had the feeling he doesn't think the earl had much to do with it. Or at least didn't wield the heavy object that ended Mobley's days. Lord Clifford is more a witness now than a suspect."

"Thank heavens for that," I said in relief. "Sergeant Scott is much more suspicious. He's the sort who'd keep all the suspects under his eye until he decided which was the most guilty."

"True. Sergeant Scott is a hard man, but like Ferguson, no fool."

We strode onward, reaching the crowds of Trafalgar Square. Nelson's column rose high in the square's center, holding the admiral aloft from the ordinary rush of London. Pigeons rested comfortably on his shoulders and also flowed over the rest of the square, fluttering away as people walked through them.

Lord Clifford and Cynthia turned on Cockspur Street, heading for Pall Mall.

Mr. Thanos asked the next question. "What about the chap, Constable Wallace? He's keen to have a go at solving the crime himself, to best his sergeant, I imagine. Wants to interview Lord Clifford himself."

Daniel raised his brows. "Does he? Wallace is a bright young man, from what I have heard. Even Monaghan has mentioned him with grudging respect. If he's careful, he'll go far."

"Should we let him near Lord Clifford?" I asked. "Sometimes ambitious policemen will coax a man to say whatever will incriminate him, whether that man is guilty or innocent."

"I don't know Wallace well," Daniel admitted. "Or that entire office, in fact. Monaghan doesn't have much dealing with them. I propose we allow the lad his interview. He might draw more from Lord Clifford than even we can, because Lord Clifford fears that anything he says to *us* will reach his daughter or wife. Wallace might be able to pry out the truth."

"What is the truth?" I asked in exasperation. "I have maddeningly few details to go on."

Daniel grinned down at me. "I will enlighten you then.

Hiram Mobley was murdered in his office in the Strand on Sunday night, sometime between ten in the evening and midnight—as far as the doctor examining the body can ascertain. He was killed by a blow to the head with something wooden, heavy, and narrow, with a polished edge that left few splinters in the wound. A walking stick, perhaps. The charwoman of the building had already been and gone for the night, and she declares Mobley wasn't there when she arrived at seven to do her nightly scrubbing. Wasn't there when she departed at half past nine, either. His office door was locked, as usual, she claims."

"All very convenient for the killer," I said.

Daniel continued. "The man of business who lets the offices next door, Mr. Ogden, noticed Mobley's door ajar when he arrived at six on Friday morning. He hurried inside, fearing burglars had been there in the night. He found Mobley's body lying between the desks, fled, and looked for a constable. Fortunately, one happened to be passing as he ran out, who could secure the scene of the crime right away. He was one of Sergeant Scott's and summoned him."

I squeezed Daniel's arm, grateful for this clearer picture. "Why do you think Mobley returned to his office on a Sunday night?" I asked. "Well after Lord Clifford's meeting with him. Was the killer with him then, and accompanied him in? Or did he—or she—arrive for a late appointment?"

"A clandestine one," Mr. Thanos put in as he strode beside us. "Both Mobley and the murderer must not have wanted anyone, not even the charwoman, to know they had the meeting."

"Or did Mobley simply return to go over his books at a quiet time?" I pondered. So I liked to sit in the empty kitchen at night contemplating my recipes and putting my thoughts in order. "The killer saw a light in the office window and decided to catch him?" I pursed my lips. "Did they have an argument, and whoever it was seized the nearest object and bashed him? If the killer used a polished walking stick, that points to a gentleman or someone of means. Did Mobley have some sort of hold over this person—wanted to call in a debt, or threatened him in some other way? Perhaps the murderer went there with the express purpose of killing Mobley to alleviate the threat."

Unfortunately, the scene I'd just painted was one in which Lord Clifford might feature prominently. Mobley could have vowed to expose his debt to the world—to his wife. Lord Clifford had already told me that Mobley had hinted that Cynthia or Lady Clifford might come to harm if Lord Clifford couldn't pay.

"Lord Clifford is reluctant to say where he was at the time," Daniel told me. "The chief inspector taxed him with it, but Lord Clifford is uncommonly stubborn."

"We will have to make him tell *us*," I said. "You say the chief inspector believes Lord Clifford is probably innocent, but I don't think Sergeant Scott does. Can Sergeant Scott have him sent to trial if Chief Inspector Ferguson doesn't agree?"

"Possibly, if Scott can persuade enough of his superiors that Ferguson is wrong," Daniel answered. "A difficult task, but one that can be done."

I watched Lord Clifford and Cynthia turn north at Waterloo Place, which would quickly become Regent Street. It seemed that they would walk all the way home.

It wasn't terribly far, but as I'd noted before, my feet were aching. His lordship and daughter would be able to have a good rest when we reached the house, but I'd have to hurry down to the kitchen and cook dinner for them.

Mr. Thanos seemed to sense my fatigue. "Shall I fetch a hansom, Mrs. Holloway? Cynthia loves a good tramp, but not all of us are as robust."

Now I felt enfeebled and querulous. "You are kind, Mr. Thanos, but it is no trouble."

Daniel was already whistling to an empty hansom traveling in the other direction. The driver glared at him as the cab passed but then he checked the horse, wheeled the vehicle around, and stopped it beside us.

"In you go, Kat." Daniel took me by the elbow and more or less lifted me into the cab. "Mount Street," he told the driver, handing him a coin. "Number 43."

"Aren't either of you coming—?" My question cut off as the cab jerked forward, leaving Daniel and Mr. Thanos behind. "Damn and blast."

I cursed feelingly for a few more seconds then decided to sit back and enjoy the conveyance. Daniel and Mr. Thanos were really very solicitous. I was blessed to have such friends.

———

THE HANSOM RIDE DID GIVE ME A RESPITE, LETTING ME exchange coat for apron when I reached the kitchen to begin the evening meal. It would necessarily be a simple one, but as Lord Clifford had discovered yesterday, simple could be tasty.

I put together a hash of what potatoes and sausage were left from the bubble and squeak and rolled the bread dough into buns. They'd bake faster than an entire loaf, so when supper was finished, they'd be ready.

Tess had spent the afternoon chopping enough cabbage and carrots to make a nice side dish, seasoned with thyme and parsley. She'd also set the supper's dough to rise its second time without me mentioning it. I was blessed to have her too.

Once the meal went up, I gratefully sank down and ate my own portion of it. The hash was warm and satisfying, the buns, with a smudge of creamy butter, perfection.

Daniel and Mr. Thanos obviously had gone elsewhere after they'd put me into the hansom, because neither of them turned up at the house. I'd barely noted their absence while I worked with Tess to finish the meal for the household, but now I wondered where they'd gone and why they'd not bothered to send word. My testiness returned.

At eight that evening, Mrs. Redfern entered the kitchen to state that Mr. Thanos and a friend had arrived at the invitation of Lord Clifford, and they'd brought a plainclothes policeman with them. They'd requested me to join them when I was finished with my supper.

Mrs. Redfern was a very proper housekeeper who did not approve of employers summoning staff above stairs unnecessarily, interrupting either their duties or their scarce private time. Her rigid stance told me she expected me to decline, but I very much wanted to be present when Constable Wallace questioned Lord Clifford.

I finished mixing the bread dough for the morning, set it in the coolest part of the larder to ferment overnight, removed my apron, and ascended the stairs.

The company had assembled in the dining room. Mr.

Davis and a footman were pouring out goblets of brandy for the gentlemen and tea for Lady Cynthia. Mr. Davis, catching sight of me, added a cup of tea for me, which was good of him.

Mr. Davis frowned in stern disapproval at Daniel, dressed in a tidy but clearly secondhand suit, who sat diffidently at Mr. Thanos's side.

Obviously, Daniel was the "friend" Mr. Thanos had brought with him. As he was known in this house and to Constable Wallace, Daniel hadn't bothered to don the disguise of upper-class twit or City gent. This was his delivery-man-uncomfortable-in-his-best-clothes persona.

Mr. Davis already didn't think much of Daniel, believing him to be a far inferior creature to either Mr. Davis or myself. Daniel being invited to the dining room, even by a welcome visitor such as Mr. Thanos, was straining the bonds of hospitality.

"That will be all, Davis," Lord Clifford said. "Leave the brandy. We'll serve ourselves."

Mr. Davis regarded him stiffly, only unbending when Cynthia sent him a reassuring smile. The footman hesitated, but Mr. Davis herded him out, closing the door behind them both.

I knew the footman would not linger to listen with Mr. Davis chivvying him back downstairs, for which I was grateful. That was not to say that Mr. Davis wouldn't return and listen himself.

"Thank you for seeing me, your lordship," Constable Wallace stated. He wore a black woolen suit rather like Daniel's, with a carefully tied cravat. His pomaded red hair glistened under the gaslight chandelier.

"Well, here I am." Lord Clifford regarded Wallace ungraciously as he took a sip of brandy. The brandy, a fine one acquired from France by his son-in-law, did not soften him.

Wallace shot me a glance, probably wondering why Lord Clifford wanted his cook present, then opened a small notebook and readied his pencil.

"Now then, your lordship," Wallace began. "Please tell me what transpired on the night of Saturday last. Take your time."

Lord Clifford's brows knit in puzzlement. "Surely you mean Sunday? That's the night Mobley was killed, was it not?"

"Yes, but you arrived in London on Saturday evening." Wallace flipped back a page or two until he found the information he sought. "Your carriage pulled up at half past six at the Rider's Club in Jermyn Street. You dismissed your carriage and driver, who put up at a boarding house and mews near Leicester Square. You left the club at about half-past eight on foot. Where did you go?"

Lord Clifford listened in astonishment, his brandy glass dangling from his fingers. "How on earth do you know all that?"

"Prominent gentlemen such as yourself are noticed," Wallace answered calmly. "As are a fine carriage and team. Your coachman confirmed that he drove from your estate, Ardeley Hall, to St. James's, with orders to linger until you were ready to return to Hertfordshire. As to your movements after you left the club, you will have to tell me. No one followed you, and the doormen at your club do not like to speak to the police."

"Thank God for that." Lord Clifford took a gulp of brandy. "I told your inspector all about Sunday night. I don't know why I should go over it again."

"I am asking about Saturday, your lordship." Wallace kept his tone patient. "My questions could possibly clear you of suspicion of murder."

True, but would Lord Clifford's answers put himself in the frame for something else? It was by no means certain that Constable Wallace would not arrest him for a different transgression.

"Tell him, Papa," Cynthia said in a steely tone. "Mama need never hear of it."

"It might be in your best interest, your lordship," Daniel said.

Daniel's assurance seemed to bolster Lord Clifford more than his daughter's words. The earl glanced at me, as though seeking my encouragement. When I nodded at him, he heaved a sigh.

"Very well. But you need to give me your word that this will not lead to more police rooting around in my business. Mobley is dead, the affair is concluded, and I refuse to be ruined because of it."

Constable Wallace scribbled a few notes in his book, as though unbothered by Lord Clifford's dramatic proclamation.

"As I am only interested in arresting whoever killed Mr. Mobley, then I agree," Wallace said once he finished writing. "Anything else you are involved in has no bearing on this case."

"I am hardly *involved* in anything." Lord Clifford huffed. "How can I be? Because of Mobley, I am now a pauper."

"Get on with it, Papa," Cynthia said with a glance heavenward. "Where did you go after you settled yourself at your club?"

If Lord Clifford were any other gentleman, one might believe he was trying to hide a liaison with a lady. But Lord Clifford was fiercely devoted to his wife, as I'd observed on more than one occasion. It was not a dalliance that made Lord Clifford falter.

"I had a meeting with friends, Mr. Jacoby and Mr. Dougherty, at a restaurant," Lord Clifford explained with every sign of reluctance. "At Wiltons, if you must know. They have very good oysters. We dined and spoke about … personal matters."

The personal matters must have been the ruse Jacoby and Lord Clifford had tried to play on Mr. Dougherty. I pictured Mr. Dougherty accepting what the two men paid him, tucking it away, and enjoying the rest of his dinner. The pained expression on Lord Clifford's face told me this was what had happened.

"And what time did this take place?" Constable Wallace asked, continuing to write.

"What does that matter?" Lord Clifford spluttered, but under Cynthia's narrow gaze he rushed on, contrite. "We met at nine o'clock. Mr. Dougherty took his leave from us at about half past ten. Jacoby and I then went to a public house, where we drank insubstantial ale until about midnight. Jacoby went off home, and I returned to the club. I will instruct the doorman to confirm that I shuffled in shortly after that hour, inebriated, tired, and needing my bed."

"I would be grateful if he would corroborate," Wallace said as his pencil scratched. "Now then. We come to Sunday. Take me through that day, your lordship."

Lord Clifford turned his brandy glass on the table. "Sunday …"

"The day the man was killed, Papa," Cynthia said. "I'm certain you remember."

Lord Clifford shot his daughter a baleful glare. "Of course I remember. I am not feeble. I woke late, breakfasted at the club. I had a meeting with my man of business." His expression turned sour. "The fellow was entirely unsympathetic. He works for the Clifford estate, he has told me on numerous occasions, not me personally. He's a stiff-necked, pompous wretch and was no help at all."

Lord Clifford must have tried to pry the fifteen thousand he owed Mobley out of the trust or whatever financial vehicle the earls of Clifford's money and property was contained in. The man of business had been wise enough not to simply hand it over to Lord Clifford. Perhaps there was simply nothing the man of business could possibly liquidate to cover the debt.

"He may not have been able to help," Mr. Thanos said, confirming my deductions. "Trusts and entails are complicated things."

"So the man explained, again and again," Lord Clifford said morosely. "I wandered about a good bit after that. Sought advice from a few friends in Town, but they were no help either."

I interpreted this statement to mean Lord Clifford had tried to touch these friends for the funds and had come away empty-handed.

"Finally, I visited Mobley," Lord Clifford continued. "I'd sent a message to him that morning, and he returned word to meet him in his office in the Strand. I had to tell him I couldn't pay what I owed. Not when it was due, anyway. I promised he'd have the money if he'd give me a few more weeks, but Mobley sneered at me." Lord Clifford lifted his brandy and took a long drink. "He told me I had to have the money to him by Wednesday—today, in fact, no later. I explained that it would make no difference—I didn't have the bloody cash. Oh, beg pardon for my language, Cyn, Mrs. Holloway."

Cynthia and I both nodded, unoffended.

"You quarreled with him," Constable Wallace prompted.

"I did." Lord Clifford set down his glass with a thump. "I told him he'd never see the money at all if he did not give me more time, and then he threatened me, the damned upstart." He sobered abruptly. "He threatened my wife and daughter. Horrified me. I'd never heard the like."

He sent a glance to Cynthia then bowed his head, revealing threads of graying brown hair that straggled across the top of his balding scalp.

The anguish I'd seen in his eyes before he'd shielded his gaze touched my heart. Lord Clifford had been genuinely concerned for Lady Clifford and Cynthia, his only surviving child. Mobley's threat must have stirred his greatest fears.

"These sorts of fellows like to resort to intimidation," Constable Wallace observed as he noted this all down.

Cynthia laid a hand on her father's arm. "Poor Papa. Mama and I are made of stern stuff, you know. And we're surrounded by people who would defend us."

Daniel and I exchanged a look. We both knew that men like Mobley and his ruffians would make certain the threats were carried out. They'd wait until Lady Clifford or Cynthia were unguarded, even if it took weeks or months. Cynthia, in particular, ran about a bit recklessly in Town with Lady Roberta and other friends. While a few of these young ladies might be good in a scrap, they'd be no match for the professional bone-breakers Mobley employed.

"How did you leave Mr. Mobley?" Wallace asked.

"Alive, if that is what you mean," Lord Clifford snapped. "I told him I didn't care for his tone and that he harmed my family at his peril. Mobley continued to spit invective at me, so I snarled some back and stormed out. I feared his men would detain me, and perhaps quiet me with their fists, but they stood aside and let me go." Lord Clifford let out a breath and wiped his forehead. "An encounter I would not care to repeat. But Mobley was standing upright, breathing, and calling me foul names when I walked out his door."

"Did you return any time after that?" Constable Wallace asked calmly.

"No." Lord Clifford's answer was resolute. "I never wanted to see the fellow again. I went to a tavern and ordered a brandy. I am not certain how long I stayed there— I rather lost track of time—but when I emerged, it was dark." He drained his goblet and regarded it mournfully. Daniel, without a word, fetched the decanter Mr. Davis had left and refilled the glass.

"Where did you go once you left the tavern?" Wallace continued.

Lord Clifford accepted the refilled glass from Daniel and took a quaff. He ran his tongue over his lips as he set down the goblet.

"I decided to visit Dougherty," he said, his voice a near whisper.

"Mr. Dougherty?" I asked before I could stop myself. "Why did you do that?"

From what I understood of confidence games, once the person one intended to dupe had walked away, one let them go. To persist would arouse too much suspicion.

"Because I knew he had blunt, lots of it. Perhaps he would loan me enough to keep Mobley from me. Dougherty is a respectable chap, hardly likely to endanger my female relations to make me return his money."

"And did he loan it to you?" Wallace asked.

"No, because I never saw the man." Lord Clifford took another long swallow of brandy. "Dougherty was not at home, according to the obsequious chap who answered the door. I will wager Dougherty was lurking upstairs some-where, commanding his man to shut me out. After that, I walked a good bit—not certain where—and then saw a hansom. I climbed in and had the driver return me to my club. I at least had the coins to pay for *that*." He sat back, red-faced and unhappy.

"And then?" Wallace said.

"Then, nothing. I went to bed. Slept like the dead. Suffered the embarrassment of the police calling on me in the morning. Seems I'd been overheard arguing with Mobley, and so of course, I must have coshed him."

"Where does Mr. Dougherty live?" Wallace asked.

Lord Clifford stared at him. "What has that to do with anything?"

"Just making an account of your movements, your lord-ship. For my records."

"It's poking about in a man's private business, is what it is," Lord Clifford growled.

"I live in Pimlico," Wallace said in a friendly tone. "I don't mind who knows it. What difference can it make to tell me where Mr. Dougherty resides?"

Lord Clifford waved a hand. "Oh, I suppose it is no matter. A house in Upper Holland Street. I forget the exact address. In Kensington."

"Upper Holland Street, Kensington," Wallace dutifully wrote. "A fair walk from the Strand."

"I was agitated. After all the brandy at the tavern, I was also a bit drunk. I took a hansom to Dougherty's, because I knew I'd never find the place on my own. Had no idea where I was when I left his street. I am not familiar with that part of London."

"Then you took another hansom back to your club and

remained there for the rest of the night." Wallace finished writing and punctuated the last sentence with a stab of his pencil.

"Yes, I told you."

"I'm trying to make everything clear, your lordship," Wallace said in a soothing tone. "All this will be verified, of course, but I wanted to hear it in your own words."

"Verified," Lord Clifford muttered. "A man's word isn't good enough, I suppose."

"This is a case of murder, your lordship." Wallace closed his notebook with a snap. "We must do everything correctly, so the wrong person isn't landed in the dock."

"My father is the wrong person, I assure you," Cynthia said. "He'd have made a muck of things if he'd tried to murder someone, leaving no doubt that he'd done it. As it is, he stumbled around London ineffectually and went to bed."

"Thank you very much, Cynthia," Lord Clifford said tartly. "Children are supposed to be a prop and a comfort in a man's old age."

"You have plenty of years left in you, Papa." Cynthia patted his arm. She kept her words light, but I saw the relief in her eyes. She hadn't been entirely certain of her father's innocence until hearing his story.

"Not if the police keep questioning me," Lord Clifford returned. "I have aged a decade in the last few days."

"Nonsense, you look fit to me," Cynthia said. "Is that all, Constable? My father should rest."

"Of course." Constable Wallace came politely to his feet as Cynthia tugged Lord Clifford up with her. Mr. Thanos, Daniel, and I quickly joined them.

Cynthia bade us a cordial good night, though Lord Clifford only nodded absently. I did see as he passed me that

Lord Clifford was indeed exhausted. His face was lined, his eyes red-rimmed.

He was a man beaten. While his current predicament was his own fault, I felt great compassion for Cynthia's father.

Mr. Thanos followed them out, but Constable Wallace stopped me before I could depart.

"What time did his lordship arrive here, Mrs. Holloway? The police interviewed him at his club much of the day on Monday, and he stayed there that night. The next afternoon, he took his bag and climbed into a cab, but his whereabouts after that were unknown."

Sergeant Scott had had the earl followed, Wallace meant, but his men had lost sight of him.

"About five o'clock that evening," I said coolly. "Lord Clifford is welcome in the house anytime."

"If that is so, why did he not come here upon his arrival?" Wallace asked. "Why stay at his club?"

So he could help Mr. Jacoby fleece a man without anyone in this household being the wiser, I was certain, but I could not say this to the constable.

"The family is away, and he likely believed the house was shut up," I offered. "I'm sure that once Lord Clifford realized the staff was still here, he decided to change his lodgings for a more comfortable bed and my meals."

Wallace wrote down my words. "Any idea why he'd taken a loan from a moneylender like Mobley?" He included Daniel in the question. "A man would have to be desperate to seek out Mobley, who had a rotten reputation. Even other moneylenders didn't like him."

"He must have had good reason," I said. "Lord Clifford might be an earl, but as he indicated, the estate does not have much ready money. He could have wanted to make improvements to the property, or to fix houses of his tenants. Being a landlord is quite expensive."

Daniel kept his expression neutral as I rattled out this explanation. It didn't satisfy Wallace, I saw from his expression, but he made a few more notes and closed his book, sliding it and the pencil into his pocket.

Wallace thanked us before he took his leave. I admired him for being so polite—many policemen were unctuous to those of the higher classes and uncommonly rude to people like Daniel and me. Wallace was even-handed, neither overly sycophantic nor overly discourteous.

Mr. Davis appeared as soon as we exited the dining room to usher Wallace to the front door. He was still disapproving —a constable should come and go below stairs, but it seemed silly to drag him all the way down and out through the kitchen when the front door was steps away.

Mr. Davis glowered at Daniel, as though wondering if Daniel would be impertinent enough to use the front entrance. When I led Daniel toward the backstairs instead, Mr. Davis stalked into the dining room, signaling the footman in the vestibule to join him.

Mr. Thanos was nowhere in sight. I assumed he'd gone to assist Cynthia with Lord Clifford. Mr. Davis would see him out when he descended.

Daniel and I made our way to the kitchen, where Tess was cleaning up from supper. We could not discuss much while the staff was about, and Daniel departed, saying he had errands to do. After a whispered promise that he'd return later, he went out into the night.

That left me at the kitchen table making my own notes about what Lord Clifford had told us, before I helped Tess with the final cleaning of the day.

By the time Daniel returned to the darkened and quiet house, I'd made lists in my notebook, divided by solid lines, of where each person involved in this case had been at the time in question—as far as I knew—and why they'd possibly murdered Mr. Mobley.

There were several names, and I could not decide which was the culprit.

"Tomorrow is my day out," I told Daniel as I brought some leftover hash to serve him. I'd held back plenty of gravy as well, which I poured over the plate after he sat down.

"Thursday," Daniel said as he inhaled a mouthful. "I know."

"I wish to spend it with Grace," I said.

Daniel quirked a brow at me. "Again, I know."

"I also believe you or I should speak to Mr. Jacoby, Mr. Dougherty, Mobley's partner if he is back in London, and also any gentlemen who share Lord Clifford's club. Members, I mean, not the staff. Can you arrange it?"

CHAPTER 9

*D*aniel was nonplussed by my demands but not very surprised.

"Thanos knows a few of the club members, luckily," he said as he resumed eating. "Mates from his university days. I remember them myself—they're not bad chaps, if vague, and would have no idea what to do if their funds were cut off. Thanos went to visit them earlier tonight to ask casually about Lord Clifford. I have not seen him since he left here, so I don't yet know what they told him."

"Do his mates remember *you* from university?" I asked in curiosity.

Daniel's smile turned wry. "No, but I don't expect them to. They know me as a friend of Thanos, which in their opinion, is enough."

Daniel had worked odd jobs at Cambridge, sneaking into lectures when he could. Thanos had noticed and offered to share his books and tutor him. Daniel had never forgotten his kindness.

I grew indignant with the other gentlemen for not

noticing Daniel, and decided it was fortunate Mr. Thanos was questioning them and not me.

"As for the others," Daniel went on, "I agree they need to be interviewed, and not by the police. You should leave them to me, though I know you'll argue."

"Not at all," I said briskly. "I told you, I prefer to be with Grace. But I wish to know every last detail of what they say."

The corners of Daniel's eyes crinkled. "I would expect nothing less."

As he resumed his meal with enjoyment, a strange and unexpected longing came over me. We ought to be sitting cozily in our own kitchen, a tiny one, with Grace and James asleep in their bedchambers in the house above us. Daniel and I would linger over supper and tea, and then do the washing up, because I'd never leave a kitchen untidy. After that, we'd adjourn to our own chamber, and …

My face went hot, as though I'd thrust it too close to boiling water. Daniel, absorbed in the meal, didn't notice, thank heavens.

I managed to school my expression by the time he looked up. I smiled at him over my teacup, which he answered with a puzzled expression.

When Daniel moved to kiss me goodnight at the back door, I kept it brief, adding to his puzzlement. I promised I'd see him in the morning, and then took myself to bed.

I lay awake much of the night, trying to decide why I'd so vividly imagined the scene with Daniel, and why it had felt so natural.

I was tinting marriage with a rosy glow, I decided as I finally drifted off. In reality, I'd be working alone in a hot kitchen with a too-small stove that didn't draw smoke well, while Daniel stayed away for long stretches on his police work.

My life was perfectly fine as it was, I told myself. I was paid for my skills, and tomorrow I would see Grace. Thoughts of Grace at last let me relax into sleep, but regret followed me. If I lived in the cramped house with Daniel, I could be with Grace every day, instead of only during weekly visits.

But that was my lot, and I would make the best of it. I always did.

———

WHEN I DEPARTED THE KITCHEN AFTER BREAKFAST THE NEXT morning, clad in my nicest frock and hat, I found Daniel waiting for me at the eastern end of Mount Street. He lounged against railings of a respectable house there, resembling the layabout many thought him.

He fell into step with me as I passed and tucked my hand under his arm. I forced my thoughts away from what I'd envisioned the night before as Daniel led me onward at a brisk pace.

"You did not say much more last night," I said as we skirted the corner of Berkley Square and made our way toward Piccadilly. "Too busy eating, I suppose." I hadn't wanted to discuss my wayward thoughts, so I hadn't said much either.

"It was an excellent meal," Daniel said. "I wanted to give it my full attention. Your sauce was superb." He kissed his fingers to the sky.

"You evade the question with flattery." Not that I minded.

"You never told me what you thought of Lord Clifford's story."

Daniel shrugged. "Plausible, all the way around. I would like to know exactly where he was wandering between the Strand, the tavern, and Kensington, and what he hoped to gain speaking to Dougherty, apart from money, I mean, if anything. I have already asked my friend Lewis to find what cabs took him to and fro and exactly from where to where."

Daniel knew almost everyone on London's streets, friend or foe, including a cabby called Lewis, who seemingly did whatever Daniel asked of him.

We had to press ourselves close together when we reached Regent's Circus, which teemed with traffic, curtailing conversation. We turned down the even busier thoroughfare of Haymarket, to Cockspur Street, passed through Trafalgar Square, and emerged into the Strand.

Not until we drew close to Mobley's place of business did Daniel speak again. "Parkin, Mobley's partner, returned to London late last night. Sergeant Scott wasted no time dragging him to the Yard. Scott didn't want to talk to me this morning, but I managed to pry out of Constable Wallace that the man swears he was in Manchester since Saturday, attending a family wedding, no less. Scott has already wired multiple people in Manchester to confirm this. On the off chance, I ducked into Mobley's office after leaving the Yard and found Parkin there."

"Was he, now?" I eyed the building ahead of us that Lord Clifford and I had entered yesterday.

"Yes, at eight this morning. He seems upset that Mobley is gone, saying Mobley was the brains behind the business. He vows to carry on, but he's not certain he can."

"What about Lord Clifford's debt?"

"Parkin believes anything owed Mobley was owed the business itself, so the debt is still valid. However, he's more amenable to discussing terms than Mobley was."

Not the answer I'd hoped for. Even if Lord Clifford was given more time to pay, the usurious nature of the moneylenders meant he'd have to come up with still more cash on top of what he already owed.

"Perhaps I ought to speak to Mr. Parkin," I said.

"God help the man," Daniel said in jest then glanced at me. "Did you mean now?"

I slowed as we approached the door of Mobley's business, but I had a more pressing engagement pulling me onward. "Later, I think. Grace is waiting."

Daniel, fully understanding why I wanted to diverge from investigating this problem, led me past Mobley's office without slowing.

Once I was inside the small house in Clover Lane, with my daughter hugging me tightly, Lord Clifford's woes, the murder of a moneylender, and other difficulties, evaporated. Grace was my world, and anything else was peripheral to that.

Daniel remained, at both Grace's and Joanna's invitation, and we had a lively chat. For our walk today, we ventured on one of our favorite strolls to the Tower of London. The castle had been both royal residence and notorious prison, and now was a place of historic fascination. The Crown Jewels were kept there, guarded by the red-uniformed Yeoman Warders, who these days pointed out the more exciting areas of the Tower to visitors.

We wandered along, trying to decide which wing had housed Queen Anne Boleyn, the ill-fated wife of Henry VIII so long ago.

"I wouldn't marry a king," Grace declared. "Aunt Joanna has us reading about old King Henry for history lessons. It seems far too dangerous to be a queen."

"At one time it could indeed be perilous," Daniel agreed. "If a lady did not bring the right amount of power and influence to the marriage, and even more importantly, bear the king a son, she could be banished. Or in Anne's case, arrested on trumped-up charges of treason. Her family gambled that she could bring them fortunes and the favor of the king, and they lost. Her uncle, the Duke of Norfolk, was condemned to the Tower several times, escaping his execution sentences by the sheerest luck. Anne was not so fortunate."

"Poor lady," Grace said with true sorrow.

"On the other hand, her daughter was the greatest queen Britain ever saw." Daniel sent me a grin. "It is why I'm always kind to ladies. One never knows when they'll become powerful indeed."

He had me blushing again. I admonished him to not be so daft, and both Grace and Daniel laughed.

"I visited an interesting square the other day," I told Grace, to change the subject, which was growing ridiculous. "Wellclose, not far from here. There was once a Danish church in its center and some fine houses, though it has lost its grandeur since then."

"May we see it?" Grace asked at once. She was ever curious.

At any other time, I might steer us to a respectable teashop instead, but my own curiosity was as great as hers. Grace had inherited that from me.

Mr. Jacoby's office was in Wellclose Square. The police did not suspect him of murder—and why should they? His place of business was nowhere near the Strand, and Lord

Clifford was trying to keep Jacoby out of it, not to mention his own involvement in Jacoby's confidence scheme.

But Jacoby had a connection, didn't he? Which was why he was on my list of suspects. Lord Clifford had gone to Mobley to raise funds to be part of Jacoby's swindle. Jacoby had known this, and had known Lord Clifford could not pay Mobley back. Why this would cause Jacoby to kill the moneylender, I had no idea, but I could not resist trying to see what Jacoby was up to at the moment.

Daniel must have shared my interest, because he guided us toward the square without hesitation.

He chose a route that would not take us past any gin houses or almshouses, fortunately, and we walked along with Grace between us, like a proper family.

As I had so vividly imagined last night ...

Before another wave of longing could swamp me, my attention was arrested by a gentleman leaving Mr. Jacoby's shipping office, which was now a few doors from us. The man wore a fine greatcoat and hat—I knew quality when I saw it. His wardrobe would have set him back a fair amount. He had a bushy, gray-streaked beard that was well-combed and thick eyebrows to go with it.

I'd never seen the gentleman before, and apparently neither had Daniel, who betrayed no recognition. Another gent doing business with Jacoby—or being cheated by him, whichever was the case.

The man was thrusting things in his pockets as he passed us, forcing us, the nobodies in his way, to press ourselves against the railings of the nearest house.

A paper fluttered from his pocket, unnoticed. Before I could stop her, Grace darted forward, retrieved the scrap, and hurried after the man.

"Beg pardon, sir, but you dropped this," she said.

The man swung around. When he beheld my daughter holding the paper out to him, smiling brightly, did he soften and beam at the sweet girl? No, he snarled and snatched the page from her hand.

"Were you trying to pick my pockets?" he demanded. "Be off, you, before I call the constable."

"She most certainly was not robbing you." I'd charged to Grace the moment the man turned to her. "She kindly retrieved what you lost, and for that, she should have your gratitude."

The bad-tempered man turned his bellicose stare on me, but I lifted my chin and met his gaze. He might be more wealthy than I was, but that did not make him my better. Such ingratitude to an honest child made him the lesser of us.

The man darted his gaze past me to Daniel. I could not see Daniel's expression, as he was behind me, but whatever invective the gentleman had intended to hurl at me died on his lips. His eyes flickered as he looked from Daniel to me and back to Grace.

"Er," he managed. "It was good of you." This phrase to Grace was uttered in the most grudging and halfhearted tone I'd ever heard. "Here, girl, have a farthing." The man dipped a gloved hand into his pocket and held up a copper coin between his fingers.

Grace backed a step. "No, thank you, sir. I was only trying to help."

The gentleman clearly did not know what to make of us. He growled, dropped the farthing into his pocket, swung on his heel, and charged off in the direction of Wells Street.

Once he'd disappeared around the corner, I pulled Grace into a quick hug. "You did well, darling. I am proud of you."

"Daniel frightened him off." Grace finished our embrace and did a little victory hop. "He knew Daniel would thrash him if he wasn't courteous."

"Thrashing is not the answer to everything," I admonished, though I secretly agreed with her. "You have lived too long among boys, I'm thinking."

"Mark and Matthew are gentle lads," Grace said, naming Joanna's sons. "But it's what happens in stories."

"Then you are reading the wrong stories," I said firmly.

As much as I scolded, I knew that Daniel's presence had prevented the man from shouting for the nearest constable or trying to drag Grace off to a police station on his own. I preferred to stand up for myself whenever I could, but I admitted it was nice to have a protector behind me.

I shouldn't have a warm, pleasant feeling about this, but I could not help myself. I was still a silly romantic, as last night's visions showed, in spite of my best efforts to push such nonsense from my head.

I took Daniel's arm with more enthusiasm than I should have, and we continued our walk.

The door of Jacoby's shipping offices opened once more, and Jacoby himself stepped out.

When he caught sight of me coming toward him, by Daniel's side, a shadow of abject terror settled on his face. He backed up into the office and slammed the door. We were close enough to hear the snick of a bolt sliding home to lock us out.

———

I REACHED HOME WITHOUT MISHAP THAT EVENING, AFTER enjoying the remainder of a wonderful day with my daughter. Daniel had left us after our repast at a teashop, his significant look at me indicating he'd be off to gather more information from and about our suspects.

I pressed the warm feeling of being with Grace close to me as Tess and I went through our preparations for poached haddock followed by a roast with plenty of potatoes and greens—I'd returned us to cooking several courses now that Lord Clifford and Lady Cynthia were in residence. Mr. Davis stepped into the kitchen as we worked and told me that Cynthia and Mr. Thanos wished to confer with me upstairs after supper.

His pinched face told me of his disapprobation. Not, I discerned, because he thought I was getting above myself, but because if Mrs. Bywater got word of it, she'd possibly try to sack me … again. At the very least, she'd keep Lady Cynthia from me, believing that I had a harmful influence on her.

"Perhaps Lady Cynthia and Mr. Thanos should meet with me in the housekeeper's parlor after they dine," I suggested. "That way we are not underfoot when you are trying to put the dining room to rights. Is Lord Clifford supping with them as well?"

Mr. Davis went colder than ever. "He has requested a tray sent up to his bedchamber. I gather he is ailing." His tone conveyed that he believed Lord Clifford was sequestering himself rather than being actually ill.

"I will concoct something to soothe his digestion," I said.

Mr. Davis nodded, still not happy with the situation. He'd been vexed ever since Lord Clifford had turned up, as he'd been enjoying his holiday sorting through the wines, free from the family's demands.

"By the way," I said before Mr. Davis departed. "Have you read anything in your newspapers, either recently or in the past, about a shipping company run by a man called Jacoby? Any sort of scandal?"

Mr. Davis's thin brows rose. "You mean Jacoby and Sons?"

"That's the one," I said in surprise.

"I recall something." His annoyance at Lord Clifford faded as he began to muse. "Let me have a think and see if I can remember."

"Thank you, Mr. Davis."

"Not at all, Mrs. Holloway."

———

I BUSIED MYSELF WITH COOKING FOR THE NEXT HOUR. I ALWAYS believed any job was worth doing well, so I concentrated on the task. After the fish went up with its butter and caper sauce, Tess and I turned out the roast and potatoes with a side of braised greens with onions, topped by a nice sauce made from the beef's juices, with arrowroot as a thickener.

A tray with a smidgen of beef and potatoes plus a few slices of fresh bread and hot tea I sent to Lord Clifford via Mrs. Redfern, while I cranked the rest up on the dumbwaiter to the dining room.

Mr. Davis was behind me when I turned from the dumb-waiter, startling me. He was in his tailcoat and wore an introspective expression, which he did when he was thinking something through.

"I did recall what happened at Jacoby and Sons," he said.

"There were no sons, first of all. About five years ago, I think, a man who'd done a great deal of shipping business with Mr. Jacoby turned up dead. Washed up in the Thames, his throat cut. Probably robbed by ruffians, but Jacoby was under a cloud of suspicion for some time. His name was cleared—he hadn't been in London on the day—but his business slumped for a while. I remember journalists writing eagerly about how shameful it was that the police presumed a man guilty until proven innocent, nearly ruining him. Instead of the other way around, as it should be."

Having said his piece, Mr. Davis strode out of the kitchen and to the stairs, leaving me with my thoughts spinning.

Jacoby, a murderer?" Mr. Thanos exclaimed when we sat down together in the housekeeper's parlor later that evening. He'd left off his spectacles, which made him peer at me. "My, my."

"Alleged murderer," Cynthia corrected him. "The police let him go, Mrs. Holloway said."

Daniel, who'd been perusing the bookshelf's sparse collection, which included a dictionary, a few of Dickens's stories, a tome on ancient Rome, and my cookbooks, turned to us. "But it's interesting that he's connected to another death, isn't it?"

A second reason I'd wanted to meet in the housekeeper's parlor was that I could send for Daniel to join us. Mr. Davis would hardly allow him into the upper floors again without Lord Clifford's invitation.

Lord Clifford remained in his rooms, refusing to leave them until he knew he was safe from arrest, or so Cynthia told me when she arrived downstairs. Her expression indicated that while she'd long since lost patience with her father, his low spirits made her heart ache.

"Very interesting," Mr. Thanos agreed with Daniel. "As was what my friends from Lord Clifford's club told me. Though nothing to do with the murder," he added quickly to Cynthia.

Cynthia plopped herself on the parlor chair, and I took the hard chair from the writing table so Mr. Thanos and Cynthia could be comfortable. I wished for tea to wet my throat, but I did not want to take the time to run off and brew it.

I left another soft chair for Daniel, but he seemed more fascinated by the reading material.

"Who is having a go at Gibbon?" he asked, studying a fat book's spine.

"Mr. Davis," I answered. "He likes the grisly tales of the more lurid Roman emperors." He'd once regaled me with gruesome details about Caligula until I'd begged him to cease.

"Reading about ancient decadence can make one feel virtuous and sensible," Daniel said. "I beg your pardon, Thanos. Please, go on with your report."

Mr. Thanos had taken the chair closest to Cynthia and regarded her unhappily. "I mean no disrespect to your father, Cyn."

"My dear Elgin, my pa lost his claim to respectability long ago," Cynthia assured him. "It is his own fault, not yours."

I liked that the pair addressed each other as *Cyn* and *my dear Elgin*. I was so pleased by this that I almost missed Mr. Thanos's next speech.

"My friends confirm that Lord Clifford departed and returned to the club at the exact times he states," Mr. Thanos said. "On Saturday evening, at about half past eight, coming in again just after midnight. On Sunday afternoon, at around half past three, again returning after midnight. They also confirm that he was quite inebriated both times he came home."

"That is my father, yes," Cynthia said wearily, as I scribbled this information into my notebook. "I doubt he feigned it."

"But only drunk," Mr. Thanos continued. "Not frightened or guilty or splashed with blood or anything. One of my friends greeted him as he stumbled in on Sunday night, then fetched one of the footmen to help him upstairs to bed. He saw nothing odd in Lord Clifford's behavior. He'd observed such many times before." Mr. Thanos flushed.

"As have I," Cynthia assured him. "I wish he could remember exactly *where* he wandered about. That would help his case enormously."

"My friends also observed a visit from Mr. Dougherty," Mr. Thanos resumed. "The exchange became heated, they said. My friends are not talkative gentlemen, and any animated conversation alarms them. They worried they'd have to summon the doorman to have them turned out."

Lord Clifford hadn't mentioned this. I turned back a few pages in my notebook and consulted my jottings of Lord Clifford's story.

"He told us he met Mr. Jacoby and Mr. Dougherty at a restaurant," I said. "On Saturday evening. I assume that is where they paid Mr. Dougherty the money they told him was a return on his investment. I thought Mr. Dougherty was so pleased by the funds he decided he'd bank them and cease with the speculation."

Mr. Thanos nodded. "This was on Sunday afternoon.

About two, my chums think. Just after luncheon, anyway. Mr. Dougherty paid a visit on his own."

"Did he, indeed?" Lord Clifford had not mentioned this either.

"Yes. I beg your pardon if I was unclear."

It was not Mr. Thanos I was annoyed with. "What were they arguing about? And why didn't Lord Clifford tell us about this?"

"Presumably because he did not want Constable Wallace to know," Cynthia said in exasperation. "But why didn't he tell *us?*"

Exactly my question.

"My friends could not say what they quarreled over," Mr. Thanos continued apologetically. "They didn't hear specific words, only raised voices and Lord Clifford cursing roundly."

"Then it was about money," Cynthia said. "Mark my words. I will wager that dear Papa summoned Mr. Dougherty to the club on his own to beg him to continue investing, so Papa could recoup his losses. Mr. Dougherty must not have been the soft mark Papa thought he was, and so Papa lost his temper. This is not a mad guess on my part— it has happened before. Papa has never learned how to gracefully bow out if a mark won't take the bait." She peered at me in sudden consternation. "Mrs. H.? Are you well?"

I had frozen, my pencil stiff in my fingers. Realizations washed over me, both enlightening me and making me feel a complete fool.

"We've been looking at this the wrong way around," I said, my voice cracking. "Cynthia, do you think I could speak to your father? Immediately, I mean?"

Cynthia's brows climbed, though whether from my

request or because I'd called her by her given name without any honorific in front of it, I could not say. When I was agitated, I sometimes forgot social rules.

"I believe he'd talk to you," Cynthia said. "Why? What are you pondering?"

"I want to ask him before I tell you my speculations. I might be completely wrong." I jumped to my feet, thrusting my notebook and pencil into my apron pocket.

I rushed to the door, which was opened by Daniel, who'd come to my side as soon as I'd stood.

He and Mr. Thanos did not try to follow as Cynthia and I swept out of the parlor and made for the stairs. They tacitly understood that Lord Clifford might grow alarmed if we all descended upon him, and I was grateful for that understanding.

Cynthia and I went up into a quiet house, no one in sight. The staff must all be in the servants' hall, or some already retired for the night. I hadn't seen either Mrs. Redfern or Mr. Davis as we'd hastened to the backstairs, but the two of them sometimes holed up in Mr. Davis's butler's pantry when the family was away. They'd sample the wines, to make certain they were good enough to serve at table, of course.

Cynthia had no qualms about marching to her father's bedchamber on the second floor and hammering on the door.

"Papa? Make sure you are covered. I am coming in, and I have Mrs. Holloway with me."

I heard Lord Clifford squeak something, and then Cynthia pushed her way inside. Lord Clifford had not locked his door, but I had the feeling a flimsy lock would not keep out Cynthia when she was this angry.

Fortunately, Lord Clifford was not abed or even

undressed. He sat at a writing desk, pen in hand. He shoved whatever he'd been working on under another piece of paper and scrambled to his feet as his daughter stormed inside. I followed more quietly.

"What is it?" Lord Clifford's exhausted and sad tones stirred my sympathy. "I wish to be left alone."

"Why did Mr. Dougherty visit you at your club on Sunday?" Cynthia demanded. "Were you touching him for money?"

Lord Clifford flushed, but he lifted his chin. "Of course, I was. Jacoby let him go too easily. I thought I could convince Dougherty to put in another investment, but he proved uncommonly stubborn. Some wealthy blokes are. Dougherty is so tight-fisted his fingers must cramp. He wouldn't budge, damn the man. I thought I'd try again that night, but as I say, his man turned me from his door."

"Your lordship," I said before Cynthia could continue any remonstrations. "What does Mr. Dougherty look like?"

"Eh?" Lord Clifford blinked at me, as though just becoming aware of my presence, then he shrugged. "Ordinary. Pretentious man of the City, who's made so much money—or his father did and left the business to him—that he forgets about those in straightened circumstances. Doesn't care, really. He made his twenty thousand pounds and left me in the hole."

"Can you describe him exactly, please?" I slid out my notebook, hoping my pragmatic gesture would cut through his dramatics.

"Ah. Yes, well. Tall, I suppose. A bit taller than I am. Tidy. Everything combed and groomed. Dark hair going to gray. Full beard kept overly tamed—"

"Bushy eyebrows?" I broke in. "Stare like polished steel? Rather rude manner to anyone he feels is beneath him?"

"Yes." Lord Clifford regarded me in bewilderment. "That's the chap exactly. How do you know?"

I snapped the notebook shut—I hadn't been writing in it anyway. "Because Mr. McAdam and I saw him today. He was coming out of Mr. Jacoby's establishment."

I'd seen writing on the piece of paper he'd dropped that Grace had handed back to him, but at the time, I'd been too concerned for Grace to realize what I'd noticed. It had been a receipt with some number on it, and I'd also made out a few words that looked like *Shires, Ea—*.

Reginald Shires, Earl of Clifford.

Why should Mr. Dougherty have a receipt or whatever it was, with Lord Clifford's name on it? I had no idea what the paper was about, but it plus the fact that he'd emerged from Mr. Jacoby's place of business formed a stronger connection between the two men.

"That is why I said we were looking at things the wrong way around," I went on. "You and Jacoby weren't swindling Mr. Dougherty, your lordship. I believe both Jacoby and Dougherty were swindling *you*. They must have been in league with each other. It was one of *them* who suggested you consult Mr. Mobley for your share of the funds, wasn't it?"

CHAPTER 11

"$\mathcal{B}$ut does that make the pair of them murderers?" Mr. Thanos asked when Lady Cynthia and I had returned to the housekeeper's parlor.

Lord Clifford, after my revelation, had still been tired but less sorrowful. He'd uttered many profanities when I'd finished my announcement, and the defiant glitter had returned to his eyes.

"I'm not certain," I said to Mr. Thanos now. "But it is worth Constable Wallace or Sergeant Scott finding out, I think. This is my reasoning: Mr. Jacoby knew that Lord Clifford liked to fancy himself a clever confidence trickster. They'd done a minor swindle or two together before Lord Clifford became an earl. Perhaps Mr. Jacoby thought Lord Clifford had come into money when he inherited the title, as so many believe those of the peerage are showered in riches."

Cynthia snorted a laugh. "More fool they. *Some* of the high and mighty are swimming in cash, but most of Papa's money is tied to the land. My father is correct when he complains that keeping up the house is beggaring him. He also has to repair the tenants' homes and pay the staff, when crops or other products might not bring in the sums they used to."

"Men like Mr. Jacoby might not realize this," I said. "They see the magnificent houses built in another age and have no idea how costly it is to maintain the drains or keep the foundations from falling to bits. Mr. Jacoby decides that he can skim some cash from Lord Clifford by making him believe they will be cheating a conceited but wealthy middle-class man, Mr. Dougherty."

"Who actually was in it with Mr. Jacoby," Cynthia said. "I begin to see. They would take Papa's ten thousand in cash and give it to Mr. Dougherty, pretending that Mr. Dougherty's ten-thousand guinea stake had doubled. But in reality, Papa lost ten thousand pounds—fifteen with the interest Mr. Mobley demanded. Messieurs Jacoby and Dougherty split Papa's money, making them five thousand each. An easy day's work."

"Lord Clifford confirmed that Mr. Jacoby sent him to Mr. Mobley," I told Daniel and Mr. Thanos. "Lord Clifford confessed he could not produce ten thousand from his pocket, but he very much wanted to fleece Mr. Dougherty. Mr. Dougherty was quite wealthy, Mr. Jacoby told him, and they stood to make fifty thousand or more each off him. Lord Clifford could easily raise the sum of ten thousand from the moneylender and pay him back with what they got out of Mr. Dougherty. So, Lord Clifford trotted off and borrowed the money."

Cynthia shook her head. "Cruel of them. Papa has always believed he was so clever, but sometimes, he's just daft."

"Mr. Jacoby played on his vanity," I continued. "When I realized it was Mr. Dougherty we saw coming out of Mr.

Jacoby's offices, it made me wonder two things. First, why was he visiting Mr. Jacoby again when he'd already taken the money and departed? Second, why did Mr. Jacoby believe that so stingy a man would be a good mark for such a large swindle? Lord Clifford described Mr. Dougherty as extremely tight-fisted, and Daniel and I witnessed for ourselves how mean he was." I was still indignant about how he'd behaved toward Grace. "Someone like that would be very careful about letting ten thousand guineas out of their sight. But if Mr. Dougherty knew he didn't have to truly pay over anything, and that he'd be getting Lord Clifford's guineas, he'd have gone along with such a scheme. He wouldn't be out any money at all, only pretend to be."

Daniel nodded. "It also explains why Jacoby jumped like a rabbit when he saw you, Kat. He must have worried that you'd returned to pry or to fetch a constable to question him."

"A constable should truly visit both of these gentlemen," I said. "Perhaps Mr. Dougherty and Mr. Jacoby worried that Mobley, who might have been in on the ruse, would tell Lord Clifford the truth. When they realized Lord Clifford was truly a bankrupt and couldn't pay back Mobley, a dangerous man, they possibly feared that Mobley would try to pry the money out of *them*. If Lord Clifford was arrested for Mobley's murder, so much the better."

"Horrible men," Cynthia said with adamance. "Papa has been through quite enough. He's a fool, yes, but not wicked."

Daniel rose from where he'd perched on the chair I'd used before. "I will consult with Chief Inspector Ferguson. I'll tell him your theory, Kat, and what you said about the meeting at the club, Thanos, and suggest he send Constable Wallace to investigate both gentlemen. That young man wants a result so much he can taste it. A real result, not a dupe to take the blame."

I'd also sensed that about Constable Wallace. While Sergeant Scott and even the chief inspector had been happy to intimidate Lord Clifford, Wallace had been gentle with him, only interested in finding out what had truly happened.

Daniel came to me and kissed me on the lips, right in front of Lady Cynthia and Mr. Thanos, neither of whom bothered to look away.

"I'll go at once," Daniel said. "I'll likely catch one of the detectives even this late but I'll leave a message if nothing else."

"Go with him, Thanos," Cynthia said abruptly, wiping off the smile she'd assumed when Daniel had kissed me. "I'd feel better knowing neither of you were wandering about by yourselves, in case these two gents start worrying about what *you* know. Thanos's friends might let on to Dougherty that he'd been asking questions, and both Jacoby and Dougherty saw you today, McAdam."

Cynthia's qualms mirrored mine. "Yes," I agreed. "Go straight to Scotland Yard and then return home and bar your doors."

"Jacoby and Dougherty saw you too," Daniel reminded me. He'd remained close, which was most distracting.

"We'll be safe here," Cynthia assured him. "I'll have Davis bolt all the doors and check that the windows are locked. My father won't stray a step, even if I have to sit on him."

Mr. Thanos was obviously reluctant to leave Cynthia alone with only her father and our servants for protection, though I could have told him that our footmen were quite robust. But Mr. Thanos could hardly stay the night without damage to Cynthia's reputation, even if we maintained that he was the guest of Lord Clifford. Mrs. Bywater would certainly be incensed when she learned of it.

Mr. Thanos seemed to understand. He pressed Cynthia's hand as he left her, not going as far as Daniel had with a kiss. Mr. Thanos nodded to me, then followed Daniel out.

They left through the kitchen, sending a chill draft down the hall as they departed.

"Very clever, Mrs. H.," Cynthia said. She helped herself to sherry that Mrs. Redfern always kept in a decanter on the side table. "Those two swindling chaps will regret that they tried to cheat my father."

"It is an idea only. We will know if I am right when the gentlemen are questioned." I let out a breath, uncertain again. "For now, we will have Mr. Davis bolt the doors as you suggested. Then you ought to go to bed yourself. You are as tired as your father."

Cynthia downed the sherry and made a face—she preferred brandy or whiskey. "I admit it is a trial looking after him. But Mama would be devastated if anything happened to the old idiot. She's already been through quite enough."

I went to her and dared lay a hand on her slim shoulder. "I am so sorry, my friend. Your father has been blaming himself not only for losing the money but for what happened to your brother. He needs kindness at the moment, not scolding."

Cynthia thunked down the glass, but she didn't shrug me off. "He always needs scolding, Mrs. H. For his own good." She shook her head. "I know he blames himself about my brother, but he's wrong. Reggie never would have lasted long, in any case. He'd become almost frantically drunk and a danger to everyone around him, including his own family.

He nearly shot me and Emily once—by mistake, he babbled later. He'd thought we were ruffians coming to murder him. When he came out of his stupor, he'd sink into a lake of remorse and be inconsolable. Everything he did was done to the extreme. I've come to terms with the fact that it was only a matter of time before we lost him completely, whether he topped himself or someone else did it for him." She sniffled as she finished. "Damned sherry always makes my nose run."

"At one time, you feared you'd be like him," I reminded her gently. She'd confessed this to me one cold night, frightening me out of my wits.

Cynthia nodded, her eyes moist. "I know. Because I am also extreme, aren't I? Putting on trousers and following Bobby and my friends to gentlemen's gaming rooms, daring anyone to catch on." She sent me a tremulous smile. "But you talked sense into me that night, Mrs. H., never worry. Besides, Thanos is a decent chap, and I don't want to frighten him off."

"I don't believe you will." I returned the smile and gave her another pat. "Now off to bed with you."

Cynthia sketched me a salute, her confidence returning. "Aye-aye, Mrs. H."

Once she'd tramped upstairs, I returned to the kitchen and fixed a tray of tea with some leftover currant scones, a large pot of jam, and another of lemon curd. I carried the tray upstairs myself, in time to see Mr. Davis shoot the heavy bolt across the front door.

"Just popping this up to his lordship," I explained.

Mr. Davis nodded without answering and moved to check the windows of the drawing room.

Lord Clifford was still awake and dressed, answering the door I tapped on. His eyes lit when he saw the scones and tea, which was not unexpected. There wasn't much sadness that currant scones, lemon curd, and jam could not comfort.

He stepped aside so I could enter. "Mrs. Holloway, how good of you."

I set the tray on a table and poured out a cup of steaming tea with a dollop of cream. "You get this inside you, your lordship, and take yourself to bed. I'll have Lady Cynthia do the same."

"Cynthia." Lord Clifford's shoulders drooped as he lifted the cup. "She will be happy to see the back of me. I hardly blame her."

It was not my place to offer advice to an earl about his family. But people are people, whether they are earls or unhappy queens or match sellers in the gutter. They live and love, worry about their children, and try to steer their way through this life the best they can.

"Lady Cynthia cares for you very much," I said. "If she did not, she'd hardly rush to London to make certain you were well."

"Huh." Lord Clifford took another sip of tea. "She knows what a reprobate I am." He lowered the cup and looked directly at me. "It is a hard thing, Mrs. Holloway, to lose a child. The Lord not only took my son from me, but my daughter. He is either very cruel or does not exist."

My own theology was a bit shaky, so I did not try to relieve him with platitudes from Sunday pulpits. "You have another daughter, who, as I say, loves you. She only wants your affection and understanding in return."

Lord Clifford regarded me another moment, then raised his cup again. "You are very astute, Mrs. Holloway." He managed a shaky smile. "And those scones look delicious. Send Cynthia in here—I will share them with her."

I silently slid out a clean cup I'd tucked into my apron pocket and set it on the tray.

"Right away, your lordship."

I left him regarding me in both bewilderment and amusement. I delivered the message to Cynthia and returned to the kitchen, satisfied that I had done my best.

———

IN THE MORNING, I TOOK UP MY BASKET, TOLD TESS I WAS going out for fresh vegetables for the day, and headed for Covent Garden.

The market was located conveniently near the Strand, so after I found my produce, I popped along to Mr. Mobley's office and had a word with his partner. Mr. Parkin was surprisingly courteous and chatty, with no sign of any ruffians nearby. Next, I took a chance and knocked on the door of Mobley's neighbor, the one who'd found his body.

Mr. Ogden, the man of business, was rushed and distracted, but he answered my questions readily enough.

From there it was another short walk to Southampton Street, where Daniel lodged. I reached the tall brick house quickly, so eager was I to tell him what I'd learned.

Daniel, unfortunately, was out. His landlady, Mrs. Williams, knew me, and after we had a brief chat, I decided to wait for him. I went upstairs to Daniel's rooms that I'd made more comfortable by adding a cushion here, a colorful picture from a secondhand shop there.

It was as I impatiently paced Daniel's front chamber that Mr. Mobley's killer found me.

e made an arrest this morning," the man said after he apologized for startling me. "Mr. Jacoby. For the murder of Mr. Mobley. Mr. Dougherty was arrested as an accomplice, though we believe Jacoby committed the actual murder."

"Ah."

It was all I could think of to say. While he'd surprised *me*, he'd not looked in the least unsettled to find me wandering about Daniel's quarters by myself. That either meant he found nothing odd in a woman who was not Daniel's wife at home in his rooms, or he'd followed me.

"McAdam was there when the men were brought in," he continued. "He told me you'd put two and two together and made out that Jacoby was partners with this Mr. Dougherty. That the pair were swindlers. Mr. Jacoby often sent clients to Mr. Mobley when they couldn't pay him. A man answering Jacoby's description has been seen at Mobley's business often, including last Sunday."

"Indeed."

He peered at me. "You do not seem as pleased as I thought you'd be, Mrs. Holloway. We got the man, or men. McAdam gives all the credit to you, though I dare say we'd have plodded there in the end. But I thank you for your assistance, especially in convincing Lord Clifford to speak to us."

"I was helping his lordship prove his innocence," I said stiffly. "He was an unlucky man, not a murderer."

A nod. "This proved to be the case. But I must wonder—if you were satisfied that Mr. Jacoby and Mr. Dougherty were guilty, why did you visit Mr. Mobley's office today?"

So, he *had* been following me.

"Because something bothered me." I knew I was unwise to tell him exactly what I'd discovered, but my curiosity about whether I was right was too strong. Besides, I heard Mrs. Williams downstairs, humming in her kitchen, and any scream from me would alert her and all the other lodgers in this house.

"What was that?" he asked.

Did I imagine menace in his eyes? Or only friendly helpfulness? I could be wrong, after all.

"How you were so quick on the scene when Mr. Mobley was found." I took a step toward the window, where I'd left my basket on the table. I lifted it, heavy with my shopping. I'd found some particularly fine potatoes. "I spoke to Mr. Ogden, who lets the offices next door to Mr. Mobley. He said he found Mobley dead, walked out of the door, and nearly ran into a convenient constable, who happened to work for Sergeant Scott. He did not say a *detective* constable at the time, but he did today. He described you exactly. Detective constables do not walk a beat, I am given to understand."

"I happened to be passing along the Strand that morning," Wallace said easily.

"Or making certain you were near so that you'd be first to investigate. Both so you could clear up any evidence you'd accidentally left behind and to impress Sergeant Scott and Chief Inspector Ferguson with your eagerness and thoroughness."

Constable Wallace raised his brows. "That is an interesting supposition. How do you know I am not telling you the truth?"

"Because you told us you live in Pimlico," I stated. "You'd have no need to go anywhere near the Strand on your way into work."

"Where I walk in the morning is my own business." Wallace's affable expression did not waver, but his eyes hardened. "How does it make me a murderer?"

"You can explain to Sergeant Scott where you were," I said. "I'm certain he would be most interested."

Constable Wallace's eyes flickered. I decided to try to make my way out, but he stepped directly in front of me.

"Did Mobley's neighbor actually see me commit the murder?"

"No," I had to admit. "Mr. Ogden only arrived in the morning, long after it was done. So you can spare him."

Wallace studied me closely, as though he did not know what to make of me. "You are adamant. Why on earth should I kill Mobley? I barely knew the man."

"Not necessarily. Mobley was a moneylender, notorious for his ruinous fees and quite dangerous. Why should he be allowed to continue his business, growing rich from lending to desperate men like Lord Clifford? Or maybe you owed him money yourself?" I doubted this last. Wallace didn't have the haggard appearance of someone deeply in debt.

"I'd never do business with someone so repellent,"

Wallace answered in disgust. "You are right that Mobley's death is no loss to the world. Filth to be washed down the gutter."

The deep anger in his voice chilled me, but I plowed on. "You must have persuaded him to meet you on Sunday night, without his ruffians, so they wouldn't overhear your discussion. Perhaps you made out that you'd be willing to take a bit of his profits to look the other way at his dealings."

"Now you are imagining things, Mrs. Holloway. I'd never take a bribe from someone like him." The curl of Wallace's lip told me this was true.

"But he wasn't to know that, was he?" I said. "Also, you are ambitious. If you solve this case, you will receive many accolades and move up in the world." I adjusted my basket. "Sergeant Scott is very careful, but you surged ahead and found a killer for him."

Now all pretense of friendliness left him. "I worked long and hard to drag myself up from lowest constable on the force to my place as a detective. I don't come from a police family, and I didn't have friends at the Yard to recommend me. I moved into my position all by myself, and I do not intend to be brought down by the speculations of a silly woman. Of a *cook*."

"I also came to my position in a prominent household by hard work," I said. "But I never murdered anyone to do it."

"You will never prove that I killed Mobley," Constable Wallace stated with derision. "You can't. Neither can anyone else. Jacoby is swindling scum, and I can place him near the scene of the crime at the time in question. He used Mobley often enough, and I made certain to make my appointment near the same time Jacoby made his. Dougherty will hire an expensive barrister to get him off, but Jacoby will break rocks at Dartmoor. He deserves to go down. It would have been entertaining to watch the Earl of Clifford stutter before the House of Lords and have his reputation destroyed—aristos are parasites on the rest of us—but I couldn't produce enough evidence against him. I wager Dougherty truly wasn't at home when Lord Clifford called on him, and he'll have to dance to prove he wasn't helping Jacoby murder Mobley."

"Then you will have to take your chances that Sergeant Scott won't tumble to your ruse," I said. "Good afternoon, Constable Wallace."

I tried to move around him, but wasn't surprised when he would not let me.

"You will come with me, Mrs. Holloway. We will walk to Scotland Yard and face Sergeant Scott together. I wonder who he'll be more willing to believe?"

"No, indeed. If I leave with you, you'll find some quiet turning or empty building in which to knock me on the head, as you did Mr. Mobley. If we stay here, and you try anything, I can shout for the landlady, who will run for a constable. The beat constable on this street is honest—I know *him*."

Wallace came at me, and in that second, he became very frightening indeed. His eyes were lit with rage, determination, and a frustration that anyone would have the gall to stand in his way. He raised his club—a long, slender thing of polished wood, like what had killed Mobley. All I could do was dart aside and lift my basket to fend off the blow.

Which never fell. Unlike Mobley, who unluckily had been alone, I had a rescuer. Daniel, who'd been standing in the doorway for the last few minutes, ripped the club from

Wallace's upraised hand and expertly twisted the man off his feet.

Wallace fell heavily but rolled away and sprang up once more. He'd had training, but Daniel had been fighting for his life since he was a wee lad. Daniel delivered an elbow to the chin and then the gut, followed by a few tight punches. Wallace fell again, this time to lie unmoving on the carpet.

"Kat." Daniel's eyes blazed with anger, worry, and something else I dared not pin hopes on. "What the devil—"

"I knew you'd come right away," I said quickly. "I saw James lurking and then race away to fetch you. That meant you weren't far, or he would have told me so. If that had been the case, I would have gone at once to Scotland Yard to speak with Sergeant Scott."

I was babbling and shaking, because I'd had no idea that Constable Wallace had followed me and would confront me here. I'd only wanted to tell Daniel what I had found out and leave the mopping up to him. I'd blurted my theory to Wallace because I'd heard Daniel's step below and knew he'd be a witness, one respected by Scotland Yard, if Wallace admitted his sins.

Two witnesses, I realized, as James came bounding in, gaping at Wallace on the floor.

"He was a bad 'un, wasn't he?" James asked me, the lanky youth towering over Wallace's prostrate form. "Not right when the police are criminals, is it?"

I tried to answer him with some quip, but my strength failed me. I found myself sinking to a chair, which somehow had Daniel on it first. He held me on his lap, and I buried my face in his shoulder and hung on.

Daniel cradled me close, kissing my hair. James patted my

shoulder, trying to soothe me, and I decided there were no two better men in the world than they.

———

"I am taking Papa home tomorrow," Cynthia announced to me the next morning as Tess and I finished cleaning up the breakfast things. It was Tess's day out, but the dear girl wanted to make certain everything was neat for me before she departed. She'd also lingered to hear about my adventures.

"That would be best, I agree," I said to Cynthia as I finished wiping my worktable.

"He's feeling much livelier now that the true murderer has been arrested," Cynthia went on. "Add to that, Mr. Parkin agreed to soften the terms of the loan. Papa will pay back every penny, but thanks to you, he has much more time and will owe far less interest."

"Mr. Parkin wants to make a go of having a legitimate business, he told me." I set out a basket of carrots from yesterday's shopping and began to go through them. "It was one reason he went to Manchester, apart from the wedding. To attract new investors, or something of the sort. I wasn't quite certain what all he was explaining to me."

"You ought to have taken me with you," Cynthia said sternly. "Wallace could have popped you on the head at any time you were walking about."

"Hardly in the crowds of the Strand and Covent Garden." I lined up the carrots I'd chosen, readying them for peeling and scrubbing. "I did not inform you because you were looking after your father, and besides, I wasn't sure I was right. I only wanted to ask Mobley's neighbor more details about that morning, because no one paid much attention to his story. I only meant to tie up the loose ends, not be followed and attacked."

"Lucky for you, Daniel was there," Cynthia went on severely.

"That's what I said," Tess put in. She snatched up her bonnet and set it carefully on her head, checking her appearance in the mirror. I guessed she'd meet Constable Greene today for another lively knees-up.

"It was not luck." I'd explained many times to both Daniel and Cynthia that I'd not have remained in Daniel's flat if I'd thought I'd be cornered there. I'd been very careful and would have gone straight to Scotland Yard had I not thought Daniel would soon be along. "Never mind. Please convey my best wishes to your father for a safe journey."

"I will." Cynthia grinned. "He's taken with you, Mrs. H. He might hire you away from Aunty and Uncle to come cook for us in Hertfordshire."

"No, he will not," I said firmly. "I prefer London, and in London I shall remain."

Cynthia knew exactly why I wished to stay in the metropolis—for several reasons, in fact. She only widened her smile and turned away, clattering through the hall and up the stairs to prepare for their journey.

———

IN THE LATE HOURS THAT NIGHT, WHEN THE HOUSE WAS DARK and quiet, Daniel arrived at the back door. I greeted him silently and set before him a plate of leftover roast, carrots, and potatoes I'd served to Lord Clifford and Cynthia for supper. I plunked a fork next to it and seated myself not far from him.

"Magistrate was not kind to Wallace," Daniel told me between mouthfuls. "Was quite unhappy that a policeman had managed to commit murder and then investigate his own crime under other policemen's noses. Apparently, Sergeant Scott had already suspected him and had been quietly investigating Wallace's movements."

"Sergeant Scott will go far, I predict." I poured tea for both of us, adding a bit of sugar and dollop of cream in both. "He has the cool-headed resolve for the job." I wasn't certain I liked the man, but I recognized his competence.

"If Sergeant Scott had a helpmeet like you, he would go far indeed." Daniel winked at me as he took another large bite.

"Impertinence," I scolded. It would never do to let Daniel know how much his offhand compliments pleased me.

As he finished eating, my ebullience ebbed. I descended into the troubling thoughts I'd had since I'd spoken so forthrightly with Lord Clifford the other night.

The only sounds beyond us now were the quiet hiss of the kettle I always kept warming and a thunk of coal breaking apart inside the stove. A breath of peace in a kitchen that could see so much bustle.

"I told Cynthia's father to be kind to her," I said as Daniel scraped his plate clean and laid down his fork. "In other words, to take comfort in the child he had left. But oh, Daniel." I let my hand slide from my teacup to go limp on the table. "I can pity him so deeply. If something happened to Grace, it would be the end of me." My eyes stung, and I suddenly found it difficult to breathe.

Warmth touched me as Daniel knelt next to my chair and

slid his arms around me. "I feel the same about James. We'll protect them together, you and I, shall we? From everything bad in the world."

"Will we be able to?" I asked, the words shaky.

"I intend to have a damned good try. Join me?"

"Of course." My resolve resurged. I'd protect Grace from the demons of hell if I had to. "Let anyone try to get in our way."

"That's the spirit." Daniel tugged me closer. "My brave, brave Kat. What would my life be without you?"

"Your stomach would be less filled, that's for certain," I said.

Daniel laughed, a warm, gladdening sound. "So would my heart."

And mine. But as it was, with Daniel, Grace, James, and my friends, I had everything I needed.

Another piece of coal broke, reminding me of the late hour. I'd need to bank the fire and go to bed.

Instead, I sat with Daniel holding me, my head resting on his smooth hair, letting myself savor this moment of happiness as long as I was able.

A MOVEABLE FEAST

CHAPTER 1

London 1884

On Saturday morning, the day before Easter, Mrs. Bywater, the mistress of the house, sailed into my kitchen in a rather somber gray frock and announced that I would be cooking Easter dinner at the home of her friend, Lady Babcock, in Portman Square.

In dismay, I yanked my hands from the bread dough I'd been kneading. Pots, pans, and crockery surrounded me on the table and the dresser, all in fullest use. Stewed mushrooms and beef stock bubbled on the stove, and the oven emitted scents of a rhubarb tart nearing completion.

What? I wanted to shriek.

I'd begun my labors on the Easter meal days ago. I had a large ham hock brined, ready for the oven tomorrow, plus a half dozen small fowl as well as a shank of mutton, all in their own stages of preparation. I'd stocked plenty of greens and vegetables to be cut and cooked at the last minute and had already made a start on the desserts. A cake with a roasted strawberry filling awaited fresh cream, and additional strawberries, along with other baked pastries, were in the larder.

My assistant, Tess, had spent hours chopping onions and celery into separate bowls for seasoning the meats and adding body to the vegetable dishes.

Mr. Davis, the butler, and I had gone over the wines both for the sauces and for serving at table, to pair just right with what I cooked.

In short, we had everything primed and organized so that I could finish the meal as efficiently as possible the next day. It would be ready for the family and staff members the moment they returned from the Easter service at the chapel around the corner.

And now the mistress calmly stood before me, ordering me to abandon it all and go cook in another woman's kitchen, without so much as a by-your-leave.

"I beg your pardon?" I finally managed to say.

My outrage must have shown, no matter how hard I tried to restrain myself, because Mrs. Bywater blinked.

"It should not be too much trouble, should it?" she asked. "Lady Babcock's cook is unwell, and her ladyship is hosting a large Easter dinner. She is at her wits' end. I had the thought: We could join Lord and Lady Babcock's dinner party and lend her our Mrs. Holloway. Why not? Lady Babcock readily agreed. You can cook a meal in another kitchen as well as this one, I'm certain. You are quite skilled."

She tacked on the flattery, which did not soften the blow. I imagined Mrs. Bywater pushing Lady Babcock into this decision as much as she was pushing me.

"It is not that simple, madam," I said stiffly. "Everything is at the ready. Do you mean for us to abandon this entire meal?" I waved at the food laid out around me. "Is that not a waste?"

Mrs. Bywater, the frugal soul, couldn't abide any sort of wastage—of money, time, or foodstuffs. She constantly reminded me of this.

"Not at all," was her brisk reply. "You will pack up everything and bring it with you."

I would, would I? My ire rose. Many of the dishes would not survive a move any farther than the upstairs dining room.

"Even if I could do such a thing, all this will not be enough if her ladyship is hosting a large dinner," I pointed out. "How many are attending?"

Mrs. Bywater shrugged. "Ten? Perhaps twenty, with our party joining? Lady Babcock's housekeeper will tell you when we arrive."

Tess listened to all this with her brown eyes wide, freckles standing out on her paling face. Her lips were parted, but fortunately she did not express her alarm out loud.

I barely contained my own. "There is a vast difference between cooking for ten and cooking for twenty, madam. Portions must be known, with extra planned in case there are hearty diners. It cannot be done. Her ladyship will simply have to hire out the meal or cancel it."

Mrs. Bywater's hazel eyes held impatience. "I fail to understand why you are creating such difficulties. Lady Babcock's cook will have already brought in the supplies for the meal, which, combined with ours, will be more than plenty. I have already promised Lady Babcock, so put these things together and come along. I've hired a cart to take you and all your dishes over, but we must make a start. Lady

Babcock's housekeeper will arrange a place for you to sleep the night so you can begin cooking at the earliest possible hour in the morning."

I nearly gave my notice then and there. Tess, her knife poised over the endless stalks of celery, obviously feared I would do just that. If I walked off in anger, then *she* would be left with a half-cooked Easter dinner and a furious Mrs. Bywater.

For Tess's sake, I cooled my anger the best I could. Mrs. Bywater was correct that I could fix a fine meal to please her ladyship, even in the most difficult of circumstances. I reasoned that, like me, Lady Babcock's cook and house-keeper had already stocked the kitchen and been busy with preparations.

While Mrs. Bywater's faith in my skill was not misplaced, I did not fancy the mountain of extra work she'd abruptly piled upon Tess and me.

Also, she might have asked me beforehand instead of rashly promising my labor to her ladyship without my knowledge. Mrs. Bywater was ever in awe of a title, and no doubt she'd wanted to ingratiate herself with Lady Babcock, second wife of a widowed marquess.

I released a heavy sigh, conveying that anything I did henceforth was under duress. "I suppose we can salvage some of our foodstuffs. Tess and I will load the cart and take ourselves to her ladyship's kitchen. The kitchen staff do know we are arriving?"

"Not Tess," Mrs. Bywater stopped me by saying. "Only you. Though of course Tess must help you carry things up to the road."

I let my hands fall to my sides, my anger renewed. "I must have Tess," I told her firmly. "Or else I shall not go."

Mrs. Bywater lifted her chin. "You are not to tell me what you shall or shall not do, Mrs. Holloway. Tess will be one too many in Lady Babcock's kitchen, and she will be needed here."

Tess sidled backward during this last exchange, as though ready to flee the house and return to her former existence of thieving for survival. I wanted to reassure her that all would be well, but I dared not look away from Mrs. Bywater.

"If I am to cook a large meal in an unknown kitchen, I cannot do it without Tess's help," I stated. "It is impossible. If there is a worry about where she will sleep, she can either bunk with me or return here for the night and set off again first thing in the morning."

Mrs. Bywater was a stubborn woman, used to having her way by means of bullying everyone with her nonstop chatter and the assumption that she'd already won. That she'd met her match for stubbornness in me was a constant annoyance to her.

I'd learned long ago to stand up for myself against those who considered me far beneath them. I might have been born in a London backstreet, but I had skills the higher-born needed, and they knew it. I was as much an aristocrat in my world as Lady Babcock was in hers.

I watched Mrs. Bywater debate which was the lesser evil —me bringing along my assistant or she having to tell Lady Babcock that her offered cook had refused to help. I might be sacked for my insolence, but I thought my agency would understand my plight.

Mrs. Bywater's mouth tightened as she made her choice. "Very well. Bring Tess along. I will leave it to you to make arrangements for her accommodation and wash my hands of the matter. If they do not want her there, it is nothing to do with me."

I nodded, pretending to be grateful. "Of course. We will begin packing at once."

Mrs. Bywater did not return my nod. "See that you do," she said coldly, and marched out of the kitchen, her heels clicking on the slate tiles as she stormed down the passageway toward the backstairs.

Once she was gone, Tess dropped her knife with a clatter and came around the table to me. "Mrs. H, what are we going to do?"

I wanted to sink to my chair, bury my face in my hands, and perhaps weep a bit, but I retained my composure. "Exactly what I said. We will gather our dishes and make our way to Portman Square."

"Won't all the things we made be ruined?"

"Possibly." I squared my shoulders. "We'll just have to do our best."

"You was going to save a bit back for Mr. McAdam," Tess reminded me.

I did remember this fact, ever so painfully. We'd known we could not be together for Easter dinner, it being a workday for me, but Daniel had promised to visit my kitchen later for a portion of the feast.

Scraps and leftovers only, of course. I'd never steal food-stuffs from my employers to feed my beau, no matter how tempted I was.

Before I could answer Tess, Mr. Davis strode into the kitchen, his slim frame animated, his hairpiece slipping from the bald spot atop his head.

"Mrs. Holloway, that bloody woman has just told me to pack up all the bottles we've chosen and send them off with you," he raged. "She cannot mean to cart off all my wine."

"I am afraid she does, Mr. Davis." I did not want to deal with his fury, no matter how justified, as I was having enough trouble with my own. "It is our duty to comply, whether we like it or not."

Mr. Davis stared at me, as though surprised I wasn't waving my knife and declaring a mutiny. I gazed steadily back at him until he calmed a fraction.

"The master will hear of this," Mr. Davis said darkly.

Mr. Davis did not mean Mrs. Bywater's husband, who I wagered didn't fancy spending his Easter in the home of a stuffy marquess any more than we did. He referred to Lord Rankin, Mr. Bywater's nephew-in-law, who held the actual lease on the London house—he lived in seclusion in Surrey, allowing Mrs. Bywater to play lady of the manor in his Mount Street home.

Lord Rankin paid the salaries of all the staff and also the wine merchants' bills. If Lord Rankin objected to Mrs. Bywater giving away half the carefully selected wine cellar, *she'd* be accountable, not Mr. Davis or me.

"I will return what I do not use," I offered.

Mr. Davis threw up his hands. "It will not matter. Once the bottles are opened and exposed to air, they will be useless if not drunk immediately. You might as well pour them into the cistern."

He stalked away after this pronouncement, in high dudgeon.

Mr. Davis exaggerated, though only slightly. I'd tote the half-empty bottles home, and he and Mrs. Redfern could enjoy their contents during their late-night chats in the housekeeper's parlor.

For now, Tess and I had much work to do.

The cakes and pastries would fare the best, if we were careful. We wrapped them in clean cheesecloth and laid them into small crates, ensuring that the heaviest cakes were on the bottom. I had to assume the Portman Square kitchen would have cream I could whip and other fresh things I couldn't tote. I put the strawberries into another crate along with root vegetables and fruits I would prepare tomorrow. Their staff should have gotten in greens and other produce, I reasoned, though not any I had picked over.

The ham, in its roasting pan, went into another small crate that I covered with paper and cheesecloth, as did the mutton shank and the quail, ready to be dressed. The stock I'd been reducing for my sauce would have to remain. I'd inspect the other kitchen's stocks and broths once I got there and adjust them to my taste.

I briefly considered bringing my own knives, as a cook grows as accustomed to them as she does her own hands, but declined. I didn't want to risk one getting lost in the commotion or an unskilled undercook ruining a blade.

Mr. Davis unbent enough to lay the bottles of wine into a few more boxes, cushioning them with straw. He carried these upstairs himself and set them into the waiting cart, admonishing the driver, who listened with a disagreeable frown, not to jolt them in any way.

Tess and Mr. Davis helped me lug out the rest of the crates, fitting them carefully into the cart. Once we were finished, and Tess had climbed up to ride with the driver, I realized there was no room for me.

"I can walk, Mrs. H.," Tess declared, preparing to descend.

"No, indeed." Tess was slim enough to perch on the small space on the driver's seat, but my plump body would be too tight a fit. "It is a fine day for a stroll. Just mind that no one squashes the goods if you begin to unload before I reach the house."

The driver, who apparently concluded we'd lingered long enough, started the large horse. Tess, clearly unhappy, gazed back at me as they rolled away.

Mr. Davis had already retreated to sulk, so I descended one final time to the kitchen, folded a clean apron into a basket to which I added a few sealed pots of spices, and donned my coat and hat.

The most direct route to Portman Square was west along Mount Street to Park Street—one over from the sumptuous Park Lane—and then straight north until I reached the square.

I had just crossed Oxford Street when a delivery van pulled by a large draft horse rolled to a halt beside me. "Mrs. Holloway," came its driver's cheerful call. "Can I be of assistance? I can save your feet, if nothing else."

CHAPTER 2

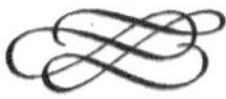

*D*aniel McAdam, his tall son James beside him, grinned cheerfully down at me, never minding other carts and wagons who now had to pull around him.

My gladness in seeing Daniel unnerved me a bit. We'd grown more tender with each other of late, but I was a cook, while he worked in some capacity for the police when he was not driving a delivery vehicle. Ours was not the romance of legends, and my heart had no business leaping high every time I beheld the man.

I strove to sound offhand. "I have not far to go now, so it is no matter. Thank you for the offer, of course."

Daniel's sunny smile barely dimmed. "Where are you heading on this fine Saturday afternoon? The markets are in the other direction."

I adjusted the heavy basket on my arm. "Mrs. Bywater ordered me to cook Easter dinner at the home of her friend in Portman Square. Not an hour ago, this was."

At last, I'd managed to astonish him. Daniel handed the

reins to James, who was equally astonished, and scrambled down.

"Portman Square?" Daniel asked me sharply.

I eyed him in trepidation. "Please do not tell me you are stalking a horrible criminal in Portman Square and that I, Tess, and the guests will be in grave danger there."

"No, no." Daniel said this too quickly for my taste. "I am surprised, is all. What has happened?"

I hardly had time to stand in the street and chat, but this was Daniel. He soon had the entire story out of me.

"Inconsiderate of her," Daniel agreed when I finished. "Mrs. Bywater is the sort of woman who doesn't quite believe other people are human, isn't she? They exist as characters in her personal drama, with no lives of their own when they have left the stage."

I hadn't thought of it like that, but Daniel's description was apt. "In any case, I must be off. Tess went ahead with the supplies, and I do not want the kitchen staff browbeating her. Who knows if they were told she was coming with me?"

"Tess is a resilient young woman," Daniel reminded me. "You have given her much confidence. I agree with Mrs. Bywater in one respect—you will do a fine job of it, even rushed in a strange kitchen with unfamiliar staff."

"Very kind," I said with irritation. "I'd rather not have the bother, thank you very much."

Instead of being contrite, Daniel continued cheerily, "One day, you'll be able to put your feet up for good. I promise."

My heart fluttered, and I admonished it. Did Daniel mean he'd accomplish this scenario on my behalf? Or only that it was inevitable?

"That day seems very far away," I replied grumpily. "I'll likely be too old and doddering to walk at all, by that time."

"Poor Kat." I read sympathy in Daniel, even as he laughed at me. "Be resolute until Monday, and then I will give you and Grace a grand afternoon out."

"I apologize for my temper," I said in sudden remorse. "I was caught by surprise by my mistress's impulsiveness. This means I cannot promise you a good meal if you stop to chat Sunday night. Though I'd be happy to see you, in any case."

As we stood on the street, Daniel did not try to press my hand, or heaven forbid, kiss me, but he leaned close and spoke in a low voice. "I will be happy to see you at any time."

My heart fluttered again, but I made myself restrict our farewell to a friendly nod. "I look forward to it. Now, I must get on. Keep well, James," I called up to the young man.

"And you, Mrs. H.," James said good-naturedly. "I'll look after this one." He pointed a gloved finger at his father.

Daniel's smile turned wry. He tipped his hat to me, scrambled up to the driver's seat, and saluted me once more before he took the reins and chirruped to the horse.

I hid my glumness as the delivery van ambled away, unhappy I had to say goodbye to the two who'd become very close to me and face a daunting task.

I firmed my resolve and trudged the final block to Portman Square.

———

What awaited me was worse than I'd feared.

The house, which stood on the north side of the square, two doors down from Upper Berkley Street, did have a fairly well-appointed kitchen. A stove of a later model than mine gleamed on a bed of tiles, its stovepipe fixed into an old chimney behind it.

Bright copper pots and cooking utensils dangled from racks, the kitchen table was wide and ample, and a carved Welsh dresser loaded with crockery stood against a wall. The flagstone floor had been recently scrubbed, and the white-washed walls brought a refreshing lightness to the room.

The staff, on the other hand, were next to hopeless. Tess stood among them, minus her hat and coat, scowling her most fearsome scowl. A plump, middle-aged woman in a brown frock, whom I took to be the housekeeper, stood near the dresser regarding Tess, me, and the crates we'd brought in vexation.

"What am I meant to do with this lot?" she demanded.

I remained as unruffled as I could while I hung up my coat and hat and unrolled my apron. "We will sort out the food and add it to what has already been prepared," I said as calmly as I could. "It is not ideal, but I'm certain that between us, we can fix a fine meal for the upstairs, with a nice one for ourselves afterward."

One of the two kitchen maids perked up at my last utterance, but the second one studied me with intense dislike.

"Cook's already got in her own supplies," the housekeeper said sourly. "Mrs. Morgan won't be wanting other things cluttering up her kitchen."

From what I could see, Mrs. Morgan hadn't brought much into her kitchen at all. One pot simmered on the stove, emitting a scent of old beef, but no other cooking scents pervaded the air. It was apparent that when the cook had fallen ill, the other staff hadn't stepped in to take up the slack.

"I am sorry to hear she is doing poorly," I stated. "Mrs. Morgan must be wretched, not being able to bustle about her own kitchen on this important occasion."

"Aye, she's in a bad way." The housekeeper nodded, though she did not appear to have much sympathy for her colleague. "Had stomachache all day Thursday, soldiered through part of the day yesterday, and couldn't heave herself from the bed this morning."

"Poor soul," I said. "I hope she is soon better. I am Mrs. Holloway, and your mistress has brought me in to finish the meal. This is Tess Parsons, my assistant. She is quite skilled and will help me but stay out of your way."

I ceased speaking, waiting for them to introduce themselves, but all three simply stared at me, the housekeeper and one maid glowering, the younger kitchen maid regarding me in open curiosity.

I turned to the more interested maid, who had dark hair and eyes and a rather square, plain face. "What is your name, my dear?"

"I'm Mary," she answered readily. "This is Jane." She jabbed a thumb at the maid beside her. Jane had an oval face, lighter brown hair, and blue eyes. Her churlish expression marred the prettiness she otherwise possessed.

"I can speak for meself," Jane snapped. "How d'ya do, I'm sure."

"Keep a civil tongue, Jane," the housekeeper admonished. "I'm Mrs. Seabrook, if we must make introductions as though we are at tea. I'll not take orders from you, Mrs. Cook."

"I'd not expect you to." I strove to keep my tone even. "If you will show me the larder, I can make a start."

"I've better things to do than take you around the downstairs," Mrs. Seabrook said sharply. "Jane will do that. Is that wine in them crates?" She moved to one whose lid Tess had loosened and peeked into it. "You'd better save back a few bottles for the footmen, or you'll get nothing accomplished. Give them to Armitage. He's butler." Mrs. Seabrook frowned as Tess and I stared at her. "Come on then, Mrs. Cook. There's much to do."

With that, she turned on her heel and marched out of the room, Mary watching her go with uncertainty.

I made myself turn to the table. I'd immerse myself in cooking—*with* all the wine I'd brought—and we'd leave this house tomorrow afternoon. There was no need for me to befriend a bad-tempered housekeeper.

"Now then, Jane," I said briskly. "Let us look at the larder."

"I don't take orders from ya, neither," Jane informed me. "I work for Mrs. Morgan. Old Bat Seabrook don't frighten me, and neither do you."

Tess darted forward. "Look 'ere, you—"

I put myself between the two young women. "I'm certain I can find my way on my own. Carry on with what you were doing." Which didn't seem to be much of anything, from the lack of foodstuffs on the table.

I sent Tess a soothing glance and departed the kitchen, turning left in the passageway to where the larder was most likely to be. Most servants' areas in this part of London were laid out in a similar fashion, and I quickly found the linen cupboard, laundry room, and larder.

Pattering footsteps sounded behind me, and Mary caught up to me on the larder's threshold.

"Don't mind Jane," she said apologetically. "She's all sourness at the best of times. What can I show you, Mrs. Holloway?"

"Thank you, Mary." I softened my tone, grateful for one friendly voice. "I need to see all the produce you have stocked, plus we'll need plenty of cream and the best fresh herbs. Where are her spice boxes?"

"I don't know about any of that." Mary stood in the middle of the larder, regarding the jumble of crates and the shelves as though she'd never seen them before. "Mrs. Morgan don't let me in here much. There's some flour, there." She pointed to a large sack that had leaked to the stones, staining them white. "We'll need that for the bread, won't we?"

I was already rooting around the shelves, uncovering bags of such dried foodstuffs as rice and macaroni, but no produce at all. A wooden box marked *Cheese* held nothing but moldy bits that needed to be discarded. I did discover a few pots of spices, but they must have been ancient, because they barely had any odor. I was grateful I'd remembered to bring some of my own.

I turned to Mary, who had her hands wrapped nervously in her apron. "Why won't Mrs. Morgan allow you into the larder? What exactly do you do in the kitchen?"

"I sort things and stir what Mrs. Morgan tells me to stir," Mary said. "Mostly I scrub what dishes she's done with."

"Don't you have a scullery maid for that?" I asked in surprise. Lord Babcock was a marquess, who ought to have a servant for every conceivable task under the sun.

"I *were* a scullery maid. But Mrs. Morgan said she needed more hands, so I was brought into the kitchen. I still have to do the scullery work. Jane is more of the under-cook. Mrs. Morgan lets her chop the vegetables. She won't let *me* near a knife, except to wash it."

"I see." I was glad I'd stood up to Mrs. Bywater and brought Tess along. "Do you have any idea where Mrs. Morgan keeps her vegetables? In the kitchen itself?" The larder was a much better place for storage, as it was generally always cool, free of drafts, and not heated by the stove, but I'd already seen that this kitchen was not very efficient.

"Don't know." Mary looked troubled. "Sorry, Missus. Mrs. Morgan don't show us much, only expects us to do what we're told."

No wonder Jane wore a perpetual scowl while Mary existed in a state of bewilderment.

"It is no matter, Mary," I said. "We'll muddle along." I'd found nothing in the larder I wanted to use and gestured her out. "Let us see what she's begun in the kitchen for tomorrow's dinner."

"Not much, I think." Mary trotted after me, still trying to be helpful. "Mrs. Morgan's been so very ill."

"Nothing contagious, I hope," I said as though I wasn't worried, but truth to tell, I was. What had laid the cook so low, so quickly?

"Mrs. Seabrook says no," Mary said. "Just an ailment. Her ladyship has been nursing her ever so kindly."

"Huh." Jane heard her as we entered the kitchen. "Her ladyship is likely trying to pry the old besom out of bed. I'm surprised her ladyship let you come at all, Mrs. Holloway. She don't like those she don't know."

"You shouldn't talk about the mistress like that." Mary darted a glance behind her as though someone would over-hear and report directly to Lady Babcock. And possibly, they would. Servants in unhappy situations sometimes strove to better their lot by telling tales on others.

Tess, who'd put herself on the opposite side of the table from Jane, frowned in agreement with Mary. Tess always had plenty to say about the family she worked for, but I had the feeling she'd be contrary to anything Jane uttered.

"I'm certain her ladyship is doing all she can," I said firmly. "Where are the vegetables, Jane? I want to sort what I need for tomorrow."

"Some tatties over there." Jane pointed with the tip of a knife to a crate in the corner. "Some cabbages too, but they don't look nice."

"I see." I bit back sharper words. "What has Mrs. Morgan planned for the meat? Ham? Roast lamb? Capons for one of the courses?"

"She hadn't gone to the butcher's afore she fell sick," Jane informed me. "So, I don't know, do I?"

"Well, what were you planning to give the upstairs for Easter dinner?" I demanded. "Boiled rice and old cabbage?"

"Don't ask me, missus," Jane returned. "I'm a kitchen maid. If you don't need me help, then I'm off." She started to untie her apron.

"No, you will stay right here." The time for friendly cajoling had passed. "Fortunately, I brought plenty of my own foodstuffs. You will help Tess sort it, and I will go to the markets and find what I can, though there won't be much left by now."

Jane glared at me defiantly, but after a time under my stern gaze, she took her hand from her apron ties. "Yes, missus," she said sullenly.

"Mrs. Morgan went to the market yesterday morning," Mary offered, her voice faint. "But I don't know what she did with the things."

Tess shook her head at me. I guessed she'd had a poke about the kitchen in my absence and found nothing of use.

I peered into the back of the room. "Tess, if that is broth on the stove, will you make certain it's hot? I will take a cup upstairs to Mrs. Morgan and ask her. I'm certain she'll not want his lordship's dinner to be an absolute disaster."

The quirk of Jane's lips hinted she wouldn't mind a disaster and possibly would find it diverting, but I could not risk my reputation in such a manner. Also, I had enough respect for those I fed to not want them suffering through a terrible meal.

Tess moved the stockpot to another burner and checked the firebox beneath, tossing in a small piece of wood. She stirred the stock, which soon began to steam.

I fetched a bowl from the dresser, which I was happy to find clean. Mary might not know her way around a kitchen, but it was clear she did her scrubbing job well.

I found a ladle and filled the bowl with the hot broth and set it on a plate, laying this on a tray with a spoon. It would have been nice to add a heel of fresh bread or a cup of tea, but neither of those were at the ready.

"Carry on with the sorting," I told Tess and Jane. "Have Mary help with what she can. I will take this up to the cook, and then I'm off to the shops."

Mary nodded readily, but the other two only watched me go unhappily.

I carried the tray down the hall to the backstairs. As I passed what I'd deduced was the door to the butler's pantry, a small but plump and red-faced man in a black tailcoat popped from it.

"You the new cook?" he demanded in a thick east London accent.

"I am Mrs. Holloway," I said, ignoring his bad manners. "You are Armitage?"

"I am." He pointed his finger at me. "You won't touch any

of me wines. A cook what wants wine for her sauces is only looking to have a go at the bottle herself, am I right?"

By the redness of his face and the broken veins on his nose, I would guess that Mr. Armitage "had a go" fairly often himself.

"That is not entirely true, Mr. Armitage. Now, if you will excuse me."

I turned my back on him to mount the staircase. I felt him watch me go, but at least he didn't say anything further.

I hadn't assured him I'd brought my own bottles, because I didn't want him absconding with them while I was away from the kitchen. Mrs. Seabrook's order that I save some to bribe the footmen told me what sort of household this was. Even if the footmen preferred a good ale to a fancy wine, they could make a few quid selling the bottles on.

Lady Babcock truly needed to review her staff and pay attention to what went on below stairs. Mrs. Bywater was apt to give us too much attention, but I decided now it might be the lesser of the evils.

I then wondered *why* Lady Babcock didn't bother herself. Most aristocratic women were sticklers about their household running smoothly, because a badly run one was talked about and reflected poorly on them. I supposed she might have been brought up to leave everything to the housekeeper and butler, but that only worked if the senior staff were competent. Even the most honest domestics would soon take advantage of a slack mistress, once they'd learned they could.

I reached the main floor then continued to the upper ones, balancing the tray as I climbed the steep staircase. I hadn't asked where Mrs. Morgan's bedroom was, but most of the staff in townhouses slept at the top, so there I headed.

This house had four floors below the attic, and I was

puffing by the time I reached the top story, the tray growing heavy.

The attic held a narrow hallway, which was obviously a recent addition, leading past the servants' bedrooms. In earlier centuries, the female staff usually slept together in one large chamber, the male staff in another, often three and more to a bed. Senior servants—cooks, housekeepers, butlers, and valets—could have their own cubbyhole somewhere or they might bunk in with the others.

At some point in my lifetime, employers decided that servants should be separated from one another and so built partition walls in the attics with doors to close off the rooms. Whether that was out of kindness or fear that we'd cause more trouble lumped together, I wasn't certain.

Mrs. Morgan had a room rather like mine, small with whitewashed walls that contained a bed, a night table, a washstand with pitcher and bowl, and a small bureau. I'd added a few things to my chamber over the years, such as a framed picture of flowers Joanna had given me and trinkets I'd purchased here and there, as well as several secondhand books. Mrs. Morgan had nothing like that in view.

She lay on the bed, her face as gray as her hair, obviously so miserable that my testiness evaporated.

"Mrs. Morgan?" I spoke in a gentle voice. "Do not be alarmed. I am Mrs. Holloway, who will be cooking in your stead. I've brought you a bit of broth, which will give you strength."

Mrs. Morgan heaved a rattling breath. She was neither startled nor angered by my presence, and she did not try to sit up. "Glad you've come," she said wearily.

I set the tray on the dresser and used my handkerchief to take up the hot bowl of broth and carry it to her. I would likely have to spoon-feed her, but I didn't mind helping the poor thing.

Before I could begin, the door opened behind me. "Now then, Mrs. Morgan," a soft voice proclaimed. "I've brought you another cup of tea—oh."

I turned to see a small-statured woman, with a face that showed she'd been a stunning woman in her youth and was pretty still in middle age. Her dark hair, which bore only a few threads of gray, was coiled and curled with the vigor of the latest fashions. She wore a gown so ruffled and frilled I feared she'd tear it simply walking through the corridor outside.

The lady regarded me with ingenuous blue eyes that held faint puzzlement, and I curtsied the best I could while balancing the full bowl of broth.

"Ah." Mrs. Bywater, who entered behind her, promptly took command of the situation. "This is *my* cook, your ladyship. I told you she'd come along and save you." She skewered me with her cool stare. "I suppose you are here to nurse Mrs. Morgan, but there is no need. We are taking great care of her, aren't we?" She added this in a nursery-maid tone to Mrs. Morgan, who regarded her limply.

Lady Babcock seemed in no way aggrieved that Mrs. Bywater was so obviously currying favor with her. "I am so pleased you came," she said to me, her voice rather childlike. "You can return to your kitchen. Your mistress and I have charge of Mrs. Morgan now."

Lady Babcock did not wear the expression of someone impatient with another's illness, so I decided Mary had the right of her motives, not Jane.

"Make sure she takes all the broth," I said, setting the bowl on the night table. "It will do her much good."

Mrs. Bywater pointedly held the door open for me. "Off you go then, Mrs. Holloway."

I still needed to know how the kitchen was supplied, but Mrs. Morgan did not seem up to discussing her inventory with me. I'd have to go to the markets and buy whatever I needed, telling the grocers to put the purchases on Lord Babcock's account.

A shaky but surprisingly strong hand caught my wrist. I looked down to see Mrs. Morgan gazing up at me imploringly. "Stay," she whispered.

*M*rs. Morgan's eyes were wide—with fear? Of whom? Lady Babcock? Or Mrs. Bywater, who could be trying on the best of days?

Whatever the cause, I could not in good conscience leave her here alone. "I will need to feed her the broth," I said to the two women who obviously waited for me to go.

Mrs. Morgan regarded me gratefully as I sat down on the edge of her bed and took up the spoon.

Lady Babcock stared at me as though she had no idea how to respond, while Mrs. Bywater frowned, used to my impertinence.

As I appeared to have planted myself firmly at Mrs. Morgan's side, Lady Babcock set the cup of tea on top of the bureau and retreated to the open doorway. "You'll be better in no time," she told Mrs. Morgan with the optimism of those in a sickroom. "And back in your kitchen soon. Won't you?"

Mrs. Morgan concentrated on the spoon I lifted to her

lips and didn't answer. Mrs. Bywater sent her a disapproving gaze, as though she expected Mrs. Morgan to leap from her bed, curtsey, and promise to hurry down and cook the Easter meal.

The two ladies at last withdrew, but I noted they left the door ajar. I could not rise to close it, as Mrs. Morgan was hungrily drinking broth from my spoon. I wondered if anyone in this house had offered the woman anything more substantial than tea.

When at last Mrs. Morgan breathed a little easier, I set aside the broth, rose and closed the door, fetching the tea on my way back to the bed.

"You're a good woman," Mrs. Morgan croaked at me in a half whisper. "Even if ya is too young."

"I assure you, I can provide his lordship a decent meal for Easter," I said. "You worry about nothing. I suppose you've put plenty by for the task?"

I didn't like to trouble her about the food when she was so wretched, but I needed to begin somewhere.

"Have a care while you're in this house," was her answer.

Curiosity plucked at me. "Why do you say that?" Mrs. Seabrook was unfriendly and the butler a drunkard, but I'd dealt with such things before.

Mrs. Morgan snaked her fingers around my wrist once again and pulled me closer.

"Her ladyship ain't wanted," she whispered, her breath unpleasant. "No one can stick her."

"We can't always love those we work for," I said, trying to soothe her. "Else none of us would find a position."

"Seabrook bows and scrapes to her, but she don't like her. Nor do the rest of the 'ouse. Used to be nobody, did her lady-ship. A tart by all accounts. Watch out for her."

I stared at Mrs. Morgan in perplexity.

I'd met aging courtesans before, who used powder and other artifices to hide their wrinkles, but there wasn't a trace of any of this on Lady Babcock's face. Also, those women had maintained their regal arrogance, confident in their ability to entice princes and foreign kings, even if those days had passed.

Lady Babcock wore fashionable clothing, and her hair was a la mode, but in no way did she resemble a former courtesan. More a woman fading into middle age, trying to hold on to her youth by dressing smartly.

"Do you mean she is dangerous?" I asked, though I could not see how Lady Babcock could be.

Mrs. Morgan didn't answer. Her grip on me slackened, her head sank into the pillow, and in another moment, a snore issued from her mouth.

Stifling a sigh, I gathered up the bowl of broth. I could leave the tea for her, but by the time she woke, it would be stone cold. I'd have Tess or Mary check on her later and bring her a fresh cup.

The tea shouldn't go to waste, however. I was thirsty from my trek from Mount Street and my frustration with the kitchen staff, and the tea, which Mrs. Morgan hadn't touched and wasn't likely to, enticed me.

I lifted the cup and took a long swallow, then grimaced. The tea was far too bitter and strong. Either Lady Babcock had no idea how to brew up, or those in this household liked it muddy.

I poured the rest of the tea into the slop pail by the washstand, piled the soiled crockery on the tray, and carried it out of the room, closing the door firmly behind me.

As I descended, I wondered if Mrs. Morgan's admonition for me to stay with her had been for fear of Lady Babcock or out of annoyance at both ladies' intrusion. In any case, Lady Babcock did not strike me as a woman who could engender terror in her servants. Her manner had been hesitant and lacking steel, but Mrs. Morgan's words had been adamant.

Watch out for her.

I'd once briefly worked for a frail, elderly, weak-voiced woman who couldn't rise from her bed and yet had kept the entire household firmly under her thumb. None dared make a move without approval from the lady's chamber. When the lady had finally died, her entire family had immediately scattered, as though in relief, and I'd returned to my agency to seek another post.

Perhaps Lady Babcock was of similar dominance, never raising her voice but controlling all aspects of those around her.

I returned to the kitchen, reasoning that I would not be in this house long enough to determine whether Lady Babcock was a quiet martinet or not.

Knowing I'd have to go to the markets myself, I deposited the used crockery at the sink, put away the tray, and took up my things, ready to hunt for produce and other necessities in Oxford Street.

"I won't be long," I promised, lifting my now-empty basket. Tess at least had been diligent about unpacking. "Start the mushrooms brewing, so we'll have a good, strong stock from them, and continue preparing the onions and leeks we brought."

"Don't you worry none, Mrs. Holloway," Tess assured me. "We'll manage until you're back."

"Why can't *you* go?" Jane demanded of Tess. "She's the

cook. Shouldn't you be out drudging for the vittals while she lords it over us in the kitchen?"

Tess's scowl instantly returned.

"I can more quickly find the choicest greens and best fish," I said before Tess could speak. "My experience is better put to choosing the vegetables than chopping onions. Which I expect to be done by the time I return, Jane. If ensuring you do the job you are paid to is lording it over you, well then, so be it. We'll have a nice repast in the end for all our hard work. You'll see."

I wrenched open the door and scurried out under Jane's glare. She was a hard one, and resentful, but hopefully I could soften her a bit before I went home.

As I trudged along to Oxford Street, a wave of near despair washed over me. Why was I bothering to put together an Easter feast for a family who knew nothing of me, among kitchen staff who didn't want me there? I'd agreed under duress because of Mrs. Bywater, a woman who, after all, did not actually pay my salary. Lord Rankin did.

Why should I not turn around, fetch Tess, return home, and dare Mrs. Bywater to do anything about it? I doubted *Mr.* Bywater would let her sack me, and their niece, Lady Cynthia, would do everything in her power to keep me at the house, I was certain.

I halted near the door of my favorite greengrocers and leaned against the brick wall, suddenly needing a rest. I concluded I was exhausted from all the work I'd done preparing the supper for the Bywaters and their few guests— which had included Mr. Thanos—and now I had to do this extra shopping and cooking for a mob. I had no stamina for it.

I took a moment of self-pity, which was unusual for me.

But really, I had been much put upon, even for one of the servant classes.

I straightened up, drew a long breath, and entered the greengrocers.

As I'd suspected, he had little left, but as I was one of the man's best customers, he always kept something back in case I needed it. Thus, I was able to at least procure some decent greens and better potatoes than what waited for me in the Portman Square kitchen.

I thanked him profusely, directed him to charge the purchases to Lord Babcock, and departed to visit the fishmonger and butcher. Though my tiredness jumbled my thoughts a bit, I arranged for fresh sole to be delivered to the house as well as another ham, along with some oxtail and beef bones so I could make soup and aspic.

A deeper wave of lethargy swept over me as I finished the shopping and began the short walk back to Portman Square.

I halted in the middle of Portman Street amid people scurrying home to prepare for their own Easter celebration and fought a sudden need to lie down and sleep.

I forced my eyes to remain open, wondering what on earth was wrong with me. This was more than me feeling sorry for myself because I'd been suddenly overwhelmed with work. Was I ill? Had Mrs. Morgan been contagious after all?

Propping myself against the iron railings that surrounded the park in Portman Square, I went over my symptoms. I was seldom ill, but my ailments usually manifested in a scratchy throat and stuffy nose, with the occasional fever. I had none of these, my skin cool and damp rather than hot and dry.

Though tired, I seemed to be as robust as ever. I reasoned

that even if Mrs. Morgan did carry an infectious illness, it wouldn't have gripped me so quickly.

However, there was no question about my sudden fatigue. It was most odd. The only time I'd felt like this was long ago, when I'd strained my wrist and a doctor had given me a bit of laudanum to ease the pain. I'd not liked the medicine and refused to take the rest of the dose he'd left with me.

Laudanum. The realization made me suck in a breath of cool air, which woke me a bit.

Where on earth had I taken laudanum?

The answer came to me at once. The tea. I'd had a swallow of Mrs. Morgan's tea after she'd fallen asleep, finding the taste strangely bitter.

Good heavens. Lady Babcock had dosed Mrs. Morgan's tea with laudanum.

Had she thought this might help the cook get well more swiftly? Possibly. Some believed that laudanum and opium were the best cure for any ailment. Perhaps this was Lady Babcock's usual remedy, and Mrs. Morgan had known full well what was in the tea Lady Babcock had carried into the room.

But then, Mrs. Morgan had eyed Lady Babcock in trepidation and begged me not to leave her.

Watch out for her.

Daniel had given me a sharp look when I'd mentioned Portman Square. He'd assured me he hadn't been on the trail of a criminal there, but he hadn't explained what had made him uneasy.

Was Lady Babcock a mad poisoner, with the police poised to arrest her the moment anyone in her household died?

I pushed myself from the railings with a laugh. What

nonsense. If Lady Babcock were a poisoner, Daniel would have warned me outright.

Lady Babcock might simply have been trying to nurse her cook. The amount of laudanum I'd swallowed in the tea hadn't been enough to send me unconscious before I made it down the stairs. Even now, I could still walk and think, the drink slowing me only somewhat.

Still, I longed for a good nap, and cursed Lady Babcock for not bothering to mention that she'd laced the tea with an opiate. My own foolishness for drinking it.

Keeping close to the railings, in case I had to hold myself up again, I continued along the street and around the corner to Lord Babcock's townhome. I took the stairs down to the kitchen carefully, balancing myself against the rather slimy brick wall.

The kitchen bustled with activity, I was pleased to see. Both Tess and Jane were chopping things, and Mary busily washed pots and crockery in the scullery.

"I managed to get some vegetables." I set my basket on the table with exaggerated care then fumbled with the buttons of my coat, which fell to the floor before I could catch it. "Tess, please start on these onions. Jane, you will clean and chop the carrots. I need them in tiny bits, to make the sauce more robust."

Jane studied me with her usual scowl, but she didn't argue.

I tried to hang my coat on a hook, missed, and tried again, my fingers trembling.

"Whatever is the matter with you, Cook?" Mrs. Seabrook had swept into the kitchen and now stared hard at me.

"Nothing." I concentrated again on getting my coat onto the hook. Almost there.

"Good Lord." Mrs. Seabrook's glare seared me. "You're tipsy. Of all the things I've been saddled with in the last week, now the mistress's silly friend brought in a drunk cook. Her ladyship will hear of this."

So saying, Mrs. Seabrook marched from the kitchen, heels clattering on the slate floor as she made for the backstairs.

CHAPTER 4

$\mathcal{I}$ hurried after Mrs. Seabrook the best I could. My coat, which had fallen once more, remained in a heap on the floor.

"I am never drunk," I declared as I caught up to her. "I was foolish to go up to Mrs. Morgan, is all. I drank tea meant for her, which I believe had a drop of laudanum in it."

"Nonsense." Mrs. Seabrook turned on me. "None use laudanum in this house. Her ladyship has medicines from her doctor, but she'd not dispense them to the servants. There's naught wrong with Mrs. Morgan, in any case. She's malingering. She and her ladyship have been quarreling something fierce, probably over the menus. They don't see eye to eye. Mrs. Morgan decided to dodge cooking what she didn't want by pretending to fall sick. Her ladyship has been contrite ever since."

"No, no, Mrs. Morgan is quite ill," I insisted. "Could scarcely lift her head from her pillow. There was laudanum in the tea, I'm certain of it, but I will be fine in a trice. I shake off these things quite quickly."

Armitage had emerged from his butler's pantry as we argued. "Nay, she's tipsy all right," he said to Mrs. Seabrook. "I told her, cooks what use wine in their sauces only want a good tipple from the bottle."

"I am not drunk!" I shouted at the pair of them. "You can smell my breath, if you don't believe me."

Mrs. Seabrook and Armitage leaned to me, prepared to do just that. Armitage drew back immediately, his tone dropping to a mutter. "Well, some learn to hide it."

Mrs. Seabrook continued to eye me suspiciously. "I'll keep silent for now. You get back to the kitchen and produce that meal for tomorrow. If I find you nodding off over it, I'll send you away and tell your mistress to give you the sack. I mean it."

I drew myself up as much as my lingering stupor allowed. "I do not tipple, as I have stated. The meal will commence, Mrs. Seabrook. You look out for Mrs. Morgan and see her well again."

"Not my place." Mrs. Seabrook stuck her nose in the air and made for the housekeeper's parlor. "Get on with it, Cook."

"Yes, get on with it," Armitage echoed. "And cease shouting in the hallways. I have work to do."

I could smell *his* breath from where I stood, and the quantity of wine on it. No wonder he'd so quickly realized I had none on mine.

"If I am not subject to ridiculous accusations, I can commence with my own duties. Good day, Mr. Armitage."

Armitage grumbled something, retreated to the butler's pantry, and slammed its door. I heaved a sigh—I'd been doing much of that today—and returned to the kitchen.

All three young women paused to watch as I came in. My

coat had been placed neatly on the coat rack, and I assumed Tess had hung it there for me. I felt a bit better already—my rage at Mrs. Seabrook and Armitage seemed to have helped clear the substance from my blood.

"I suggest we ignore further interruptions," I instructed. "We have much to accomplish. Jane, when you've done the carrots, I'll show you how to store the greens to keep them fresh for tomorrow."

As both maids bent over their tasks, I stepped to the sink in the scullery and seized the cup I'd taken from Mrs. Morgan's room before Mary could drop it into the sudsy water.

Mary regarded me with perplexity, but I hurried past her back to the kitchen, surreptitiously sliding the cup into a drawer in the dresser.

I moved to the table and began to sort what was in the basket, but my legs trembled, and I had to sit down quickly to do it.

———

SOMEHOW, WE MANAGED TO FINISH OUR PREPARATIONS THAT afternoon, Tess and I recreating what we'd done in my kitchen and carefully storing the pastries and tarts we'd brought with us.

I mixed bread dough and kneaded it, letting it rise for baking in the morning, plus broke off a small piece to roll into buns for the kitchen staff's supper that night.

Apparently, a meal wasn't required for the household that evening, as his lordship and his son, Lord Alfred Charlton, had gone to their club. Lady Babcock was out with her step-daughter, Lady Margaret, who was quite a beauty and would likely marry anyone she chose, according to Mary. Only the staff needed to be fed, and I knew I could prepare a good supper for us all.

As I worked on this and tomorrow's feast, I felt much better, the effects of the laudanum wearing off. I wasn't certain what I'd do with the unwashed cup I'd hidden, but it was evidence I hadn't muddled my head with drink.

Mary, who'd quickly grown comfortable with me and Tess, chattered away about Lord Babcock and his family. It was common knowledge that Lady Babcock was his lordship's second wife, and that the son and daughter of the household, both in their twenties, were children of the marquess and his first wife.

Lord Alfred was being groomed to step into the marquess's shoes whenever Lord Babcock popped off. Lady Margaret, as Mary had mentioned, was quite beautiful and had any number of suitors. Lady Margaret sometimes came down to the kitchen, sweet as you please, to ask for a dish to be made for tea with her friends, or to snatch a tidbit, as she'd been doing since she was a child.

Mary had no use at all for the second Lady Babcock. It seemed no one did, though she'd been Lord Babcock's wife for the past twenty years.

I did not condone gossiping in the kitchen, but I admit I didn't stop Tess asking questions. Nor did I make myself not listen to the answers.

"Lord Alfred will likely toss her ladyship out on her ear when he inherits," Mary said with confidence. "Stands to reason. She ain't their mum, is she?"

"Is Lord Babcock likely to fall off his perch any time soon?" Tess asked with unfeigned curiosity.

"Could be," Mary said. "He's seventy, if he's a day."

"That's no great age," I said as I competently rolled out dough for the buns and tucked the edges under. "Not in these times. Patent medicines can do wonders."

"Lord Alfred loves his dad, that's for certain," Mary went on. "Is ever so gentle with him."

Jane, who'd listened to much of the conversation in sullen silence, let out a snort. "That ain't true. Lord Alfred wants to be marquess, not just a marquess's son."

"Lord Alfred is too kind for that," Mary said insistently. From the flush on her cheek, I deduced she had a fondness for Lord Alfred.

"You think the best of everybody, Mary," Jane sneered. "'Cause you're a fool."

"Now, Jane, mind your tongue," I admonished. I agreed with her that Mary was a bit too quick to trust, but Jane's philosophy seemed to be to dislike everyone on sight.

I wondered what had happened to give Jane such anger. The likes of us had to drudge for a living, and while some complained, others did it cheerfully and managed to live a happy life. I concluded that more than hard labor had turned Jane bitter.

"Lord Babcock must have had his children later in life," I mused. "If Lord Alfred and Lady Margaret are not yet thirty."

"His first wife had trouble carrying little ones," Mary said. "Lost a few before Lord Alfred and Lady Margaret came along, and it was touch and go with both of them. That's how the first Lady Babcock died, so it's said. Trying for another child."

"How very sad," I said in sudden sympathy. "That must have been difficult for the family."

"That's not what *everyone* says," Jane broke in with a scowl at Mary. "Some say Lord Babcock poisoned the first Lady

Babcock so he could marry the second one. She was young then, quite a beauty in her day, I'm told."

"A lady who miscarried children and had trouble bearing them likely was weakened by it," I said. "It is not surprising that the first Lady Babcock died. Not every death is helped along by poison, even if it might seem unexpected. A person's constitution can be a complicated thing."

My mother had been a robust woman, but working so hard to keep us in bread and butter, not to mention the rent for our tiny rooms, had worn her down. When her illness came, she hadn't had any strength left to fight it.

I busily formed more rolls, willing my eyes to remain dry.

"What about your patent medicines that keep a body fit?" Jane asked with sarcasm.

I sent her an admonishing frown, both in disapproval and to disguise my emotions. "Do not be so impertinent, Jane. Have you finished with those carrots?"

Jane shoved a plate of them to me, cut into a perfect dice. I admit, the reason I didn't send Jane off on errands that would get her out of the kitchen was that she was proving quite competent at her job.

Mary, on the other hand, fumbled even at stirring a batter, more interested in chattering. I kept her sorting and stacking dishes and pans when she wasn't washing them. Mostly, she rested her hip against the table and talked while we worked.

"Excellent," I told Jane. "Now please do the same with the parsnips. They'll make a fine addition to the ham."

Jane made a face at me but fell to chopping once more.

———

WHEN I SERVED THE STAFF THEIR SUPPER THAT NIGHT, I observed a softening in belligerence toward me. The three footmen shoveled in the pork, potatoes, and soft buns slathered in butter with great enjoyment, and even Mrs. Seabrook gave me a grudging, *I suppose you do know something about cooking.*

I did not hear from Armitage, who snatched a plate and shut himself in his butler's pantry, but the dish that Mary brought back from him had been scraped clean.

Jane said nothing at all as we ate our meal in the kitchen, but she ceased glowering at me and helped herself to two buns.

After we finished, I took a basket of food scraps up to the street, as was my habit, to give to any lingering beggars.

To my surprise, the men and women who usually waited for me outside the Mount Street house had turned up here. Word had spread of my whereabouts, I supposed.

After I'd emptied the basket, I walked a little way down the road to a figure who huddled beneath a tree near the railings to the square's park.

"I suppose you've come to look after me," I said to the motionless lump. "And told these others to as well."

Daniel unfolded to his full height, shrugging off the tattered blanket he'd pulled around his shoulders. "I will always look out for you, Kat."

I did not like the warmth that filled me at his words. I kept my tone brisk. "If you wish to be useful, will you find something out for me?" I pulled the cup I'd hidden from the bottom of the basket. "Will you have someone test the substance in here for me? I believe it is only laudanum, but I want to be certain."

CHAPTER 5

*D*aniel's nonchalance faded in an instant. "Why?" he asked, tone sharp.

"Someone dosed the cook. I want to know whether it was out of concern for her health or something more sinister."

Daniel took the cup and peered at the dregs inside, though he could scarcely see them in this light. "Why would someone want to poison the cook?"

"I don't know, do I?" I demanded. "That is why I wish to be certain. Her ladyship—or whoever prepared the tea—perhaps wished to aid her to rest. My fancy might be wrong."

"Your ideas usually aren't wrong." Daniel folded a handkerchief around the cup and tucked it into his pocket. "I will have this looked at right away and tell you the results tomorrow." He put a hand on my arm. "I don't like you in a house where people are dropping laudanum into teacups on a whim."

"Do not worry—I am careful." I decided I would not upset him with the fact that I'd discovered the doctored tea by drinking it myself. "Who on earth will you have test the substance late on the Saturday night before Easter?"

Daniel shrugged. "I know a number of men for whom one day is the same as another. Thanos, for instance, will break into a chemical lab at the Polytechnic if I ask him to."

"He mustn't get into any trouble," I said quickly. "He was invited to Easter dinner with Lady Cynthia and the Bywaters, though I do not know if the invitation will extend to him coming to Lord Babcock's meal. Rather unfair." My annoyance at the situation resurged.

"I doubt he'll mind." Daniel flashed a smile. "His greatest disappointment would be not dining with Lady Cynthia, but he'll mend."

"It was highly inconvenient to all of us," I growled. "But never mind. What's done is done. I will prepare a fine dinner and then go home."

"After you discover why the cook was given laudanum, of course." Daniel's eyes twinkled in the faint gaslight from the road.

I frowned at him. "Do go away if you will only tease me."

Daniel laughed, which loosened me enough to smile back at him.

He ceased his laughter abruptly, stepped to me, and caught my mouth in a kiss.

I was too surprised to stop him, and truth to tell, I did not want to. I savored the warmth of it until Daniel eased back and regarded me with an unreadable look.

"Good night, Kat," he said softly.

"Good night, Daniel." I quickly turned and took my leave before I'd be tempted to stay.

———

I slept that night in a tiny room next to the butler's pantry, which had obviously once been used for storing wine and other foodstuffs. The wine bottles were gone, but their racks remained, a bunk shoved into the narrow space between them. The nook was set up for when extra help was needed in the house, Mrs. Seabrook explained to me.

There was no room for Tess. Mary offered to let her bunk in with herself, Jane, and a downstairs maid, but Jane made her disapprobation known.

"I can barely sleep with you two kicking me," Jane told Mary. "I don't need a third pair of feet at me."

"Tess can return to Mount Street for the night and walk back in the morning," I intervened. "It is no great distance."

That was true, but the night had grown dark, and Tess glanced nervously at the high windows. I helped her into her coat and guided her to the back door.

"Daniel is lurking," I whispered to her. "He'll see you home safe."

Tess brightened at my words. "I'll be here first thing," she promised before she slipped out.

I hoped she'd treat herself to a good long rest, which was more than I'd obtain on the lumpy cot.

I was proved correct about the bed's discomfort. I woke very early in the morning, out of sorts, but washed my face and hands, donned my clothes and apron, and entered the kitchen ready to work.

No one was stirring yet, and I got much done before the others, including Tess, arrived an hour later. Mary and Jane were surprised that I had bread baking and hash frying for our breakfast, as well as the ham basted and ready for the oven. Tess, used to my morning efficiency, simply hung up her hat and tied on her apron.

"Daniel has news for you," Tess murmured to me when we had a moment alone.

"Is he outside?" I hoped so. A chat with Daniel would be a refreshing reprieve in an otherwise hectic morning.

Tess shook her head. "He says that nice Mr. Thanos is coming to dinner, and he'll tell you."

"Good." I was disappointed I wouldn't be able to rush up to the street and confer with Daniel, but I'd be glad to see Mr. Thanos. I was also happy he'd not be cheated out of his Easter dinner.

I had little time to ponder about what Mr. Thanos might have to say. After a quick repast, we cooked breakfast for those upstairs before continuing with the main meal of the day.

Breakfast for those above stairs meant plenty of fresh bread, toasted muffins with butter, a tureen of poached eggs, and some of the potato hash I'd made for the staff. A tray with a small amount of all of this went up via Mrs. Seabrook to the lady of the house for breakfast in bed, while the rest of the family would help themselves from the dishes at the sideboard.

Mrs. Seabrook paused to study the tray I'd prepared for Lady Babcock. "It looks edible," she said. She hadn't yet sampled any breakfast, declaring it was her duty to serve her ladyship first.

"It's delicious, Mrs. Seabrook," Mary assured her. "At least the hash and the bread. Mrs. Holloway is a fine cook."

Mrs. Seabrook glanced at Jane, who was less likely to gush at everything. "Best breakfast I've et in a good bit," she said grudgingly.

Mrs. Seabrook lifted her brows but said nothing more as she continued out with the tray.

I set Jane to slicing potatoes Mary had diligently scrubbed, while Tess and I washed and tore apart the greens, which we'd keep crisp in water until they were served. I slid the ham from the oven to add the carrots, onions, parsnips, and celery to the juices and set it all back in to continue roasting alongside the shank of mutton. The quail, which would take less time to roast, I dressed and added to the oven. As there were only six of them, these would have to be sliced apart to be shared as small servings.

The fish I'd ordered had been delivered, as fishermen, like domestics, were unable to take many holidays. In addition to the ham, mutton, and quail, we'd have the first courses of oxtail soup and poached sole, then croquettes with a soubise sauce, which was a white sauce seasoned with cayenne and onions, to which I added a bit of bacon for a smoky flavor.

For the desserts, I set Mary to whipping cream—something uncomplicated for her—which I then sweetened with a touch of sugar. I sliced the strawberries myself to set on the cake that had survived the journey from Mount Street.

The pastries also needed to be iced, the ham basted, and stocks made into gravies and sauces. We bustled from table to oven to dresser and back, while Mary, once she'd whipped the cream to perfection, carried loads of pots and dishes to her sink in the scullery.

Mrs. Seabrook returned. "Her ladyship devoured her breakfast," she declared. "First time in a long while."

I was pleased she liked it. "How is Mrs. Morgan?" I'd sent a bit of hash and toasted muffin upstairs via Mary earlier, and she'd said the cook was awake though still weak.

"Too much to do this morning to look in on her," Mrs. Seabrook snapped and marched out, though she slid the plate of food I'd prepared for her from the table as she went.

We soon heard the slam of the door to the housekeeper's parlor.

I was far too busy to look in on Mrs. Morgan myself, but I told Mary to nip upstairs and retrieve the tray. I'd put a hearty cup of tea, one without laudanum, on it, with instructions to Mary that the cook was not to drink or eat anything that I didn't send her myself.

Mary returned while Tess was removing another fresh-baked loaf from the oven, the bread's odor inviting.

"Cook et it all." Mary showed me the tray with its empty plates. "She's feeling a bit better, but I don't think she'll be down to help us today."

That was just as well, I decided. Two strong-minded cooks in one kitchen simply got in each other's way.

"She says she wants to have a chat with you soon," Mary went on. "She's worried about the dinner, I think."

We were well into the most critical parts of the meal, everything needing to come together in a moment, so I could not rush upstairs and reassure Mrs. Morgan right now. I'd wait until the last course went upstairs, then I'd take her a piece of strawberry cake and tell her that all was well.

I was pleased that we'd begun moving like a well-oiled machine, differences put aside in the rush to finish the meal. Even Jane ceased her antagonism and quietly chopped, stirred, and iced what I put in front of her. Tess was invaluable with her knowledge of what needed to be tended first, which she'd learned in her years of working for me.

Mary, who left her sink from time to time to scurry halfway up the outside stairs, reported on the guests' arrivals.

"There's that pretty Lady Cynthia, with her aunt and uncle," Mary announced when she descended. "I hear she wears trousers, but she's in a frock like anyone else." She sounded disappointed. "A black-haired man came with them. Maybe her sweetheart?"

Mr. Thanos, I thought in relief. Mrs. Bywater hadn't, in the end, stopped him coming. Mr. Thanos got along well with almost everyone, so I didn't worry about him much.

Other guests included a bishop in a purple waistcoat and dog collar, one of the Babcocks' cousins, a few ladies and gentlemen who were friends of Lord Alfred and Lady Margaret, and Lady Babcock's maiden aunt. *A commoner,* Mrs. Seabrook sniffed on her way through. *Nobody.*

Mr. and Mrs. Bywater were commoners as well, I reflected, but they were blood related to a daughter of an earl, so perhaps they were spared Mrs. Seabrook's complete disdain. I'd already heard Mrs. Seabrook refer to Mrs. Bywater as *Lady Babcock's silly friend,* which meant she didn't think much of her, in any case.

Mrs. Seabrook said that the guests would converse in the drawing room with whatever drinks Lord Babcock served them, then they'd move to the dining room.

In the kitchen, we hurriedly put the soup into the dumb-waiter, and I cranked it upstairs to where Armitage, who'd slid into a frock coat and hurried up a quarter of an hour ago, would be poised to retrieve it.

The fish went up soon after, and then the ham came out of the oven in all its glory.

I refused to let the others help me transfer it to the large platter that would be its final resting place. I settled the platter on a tray then added roasted potatoes, spring cherries in aspic, and a pot of the jelly sauce that would accompany it all.

I carried the tray carefully to the dumbwaiter, while Tess, Mary, and Jane watched proudly. I had just slid the ham and its trimmings into the dumbwaiter's box and shut its door when Mrs. Seabrook hastened into the kitchen.

"Put it all away," Mrs. Seabrook commanded. "The dinner is off."

I froze with my fingers around the dumbwaiter's door handle, certain I hadn't heard her aright. Tess and Jane fell equally silent behind me. The outburst, when it came, was from Mary.

"What d'ya mean it's off?" she screeched. "We worked ever so hard. I scrubbed all them tatties!"

I heard Mrs. Seabrook's swift movement and swung around in time to seize her upraised arm before she could strike Mary, who flinched away from her.

"What has happened?" I demanded, releasing the indignant Mrs. Seabrook. At least she let her hand fall and did not try again to hit Mary. "A family does not dismiss an entire meal on a whim, especially not on a feast day. Is someone ill?"

Mrs. Seabrook drew herself up. "Lord Alfred has died," she told me in a hard voice.

The four of us stared at her in shock. Mrs. Seabrook's eyes were red-rimmed, and her breath came fast.

Died? I repeated to myself. Lord Alfred, the marquess's heir, was a young man, as Mary had informed us.

Mary gasped in stunned dismay. "His young lordship? Can't be. You've made a mistake."

Mrs. Seabrook rounded on her as though she'd box Mary's ears, but fortunately, she did no such thing. "It is not a mistake, you stupid girl. He is dead, and his lordship has canceled the meal."

"Poor man." Tess was the only one of us jarred out of our amazement to express sympathy. "Was he sickly? Or frail? Sometimes people just fall over, like, no matter how young."

"He weren't frail." Mary scoffed. "His young lordship is robust and hearty. Rides every morning, don't he? So handsome, always with a kind word for me. It must have been the fish." Her voice broke, and she buried her face in her apron and began to weep.

"It was *not* the fish," I said immediately. Cooks were prone to be the first blamed when someone grew peaky over their supper. "It was delivered fresh, and I checked it thoroughly. It was sweet as can be. I taste every dish before it's plated, and I am right as rain."

"He never ate the fish, you silly woman," Mrs. Seabrook snapped. "He was wandering about the hall as they all went into dine, telling me his stomach was a bit achy and that the others should begin without him. I was clearing up in the drawing room when I heard the front door open, but no one was announced. When I came out to see who the footman had admitted, I found the door wide open and Lord Alfred dead on the floor."

Mrs. Seabrook drew a sharp breath, as though the impact of finding him was just coming to her. She needed a strong cup of tea, though I was too dazed to pour her one at the moment.

Mary continued to sob, but Jane was utterly still, her face draining of color until it was nearly green.

"Did his heart give out?" Tess asked gently. "I had a cousin who swore he was only dyspeptic one day, but he died that evening, sleeping in a chair by the fire."

"I doubt it," Mrs. Seabrook retorted. "He was stabbed, wasn't he? A tramp, who'd been skulking about outside all night, came right into our house and struck him with a knife. Now, take away all this food, Mrs. Holloway. We won't be needing it."

CHAPTER 6

As soon as Mrs. Seabrook marched out of the kitchen, the three kitchen maids began to babble simultaneously.

"Is it really true?" Mary scrubbed her face with her apron. "Should we run for a constable?"

"A constable, yes, if he were murdered," Tess said. "I can go." I knew she meant to seek Caleb, who would be on his beat around Mount Street today.

"It were never a tramp that killed him." This last came from Jane, who still appeared rather sickly.

"Why do you say that, Jane?" I asked.

Jane shrugged, her sullenness returning. "Why should a tramp march inside and stick a knife into the first person he sees?"

"Because he's a madman," Mary wailed. "Poor Lord Alfred. We ain't safe here, not if they could do that to the poor young master." Her sobs continued.

"Mary." I made my voice cut through her hysteria. "Take the rest of the rolls from the oven before they burn. Use the towels so you don't scorch your hands and set the pan on top of the stove. Jane, carry the ham back to the table. We'll divide up the vegetables among us staff, because they won't last, and we'll send up the aspic and slices of ham to put on the sideboard in the dining room. The family will be hungry, even through this tragedy. Tess, please go out and find Mr. McAdam and tell him what's happened."

I assumed the tramp Mrs. Seabrook claimed had been lurking all night was Daniel. Why he had nothing better to do than linger in Portman Square, I did not know, but I was grateful he'd remained.

"Who's Mr. McAdam?" Jane asked in sudden suspicion.

"Someone who might be able to help. Take care with that tray, Jane. It is heavy."

"I know that." Jane's lip curled as she carried the ham to the table, but she was cautious while crossing the floor. She set down the ham amid the pile of cakes and pastries we'd readied. "What's going to become of it all? Mary ain't wrong. We worked our fingers to the bone."

I watched Tess remove her apron and scuttle out, wishing I could go with her. "It sometimes happens, unfortunately," I said to Jane. "We will store what we can for the family to eat, though I'm certain my mistress will insist that anything we brought returns with us."

"Sounds like your mistress is a right cow," Jane declared.

A light female voice answered her. "That is possibly true."

Jane swung around, her face going scarlet as Lady Cynthia walked briskly into the kitchen.

Cynthia surveyed our mess and shook her head in sympathy. "My, my, what a waste. You are quite right, Mrs. H. Auntie sent me down here to tell you we must pack up all the food and wine and take it home to Mount Street. Not one morsel to be missed, she said."

Jane dropped a contrite curtsey. "Sorry, my lady."

"Quite all right," Lady Cynthia said. "That is Auntie all over, isn't it? Also, I'm dying of hunger. The soup was tasty, but I barely had a bite before Lady Babcock lays down her spoon and tells the footmen to serve the fish. Had maybe two bites of that before Mrs. Seabrook raised the alarm about poor Alfred. I thought Lady Babcock would faint dead away, but the rest of the family and guests ignored her in their stampede to the hall. Lord Babcock is beside himself with grief, as you can imagine, but he's resisting sending for the police, saying it will do no good."

"Please sit down, my lady." I gestured Cynthia to the least cluttered corner of the table and drew the best chair to it. I took up my knife and sliced a few pieces of ham for her and fetched one of the buns Mary had just removed from the oven. "Tuck into that," I told her as I set the plate in front of her and spooned sauce over all. "Tess has gone to tell Daniel."

"Good for her." Cynthia snatched up a fork with enthusiasm. "You don't mind if Thanos comes down as well, do you? He's hovering at the top of the stairs, uncertain of his welcome in the kitchen but not wanting to intrude on the family either. I had the excuse of Auntie to enter your sanctuary."

This kitchen was hardly a sanctuary, but I knew what Cynthia meant. I sliced off a few more pieces of ham. "Of course he is welcome."

"Excellent. I'll fetch him."

"No need," I said quickly as she started to rise. "I will invite him down. You enjoy your meal."

Cynthia settled in again and lifted her fork. "Don't mind

if I do. I feel terrible wanting to eat when someone has just killed poor Alfred, but for some reason I'm famished. Excellent ham, Mrs. H."

Jane watched Lady Cynthia in some trepidation, Mary peeking in from the scullery to which she'd retreated.

I thanked Cynthia for her compliment then hastened to the backstairs and up them. I wanted to tow Mr. Thanos to the kitchen before Mrs. Seabrook or Armitage saw him and chivvied him somewhere, possibly out of the house.

When I opened the green baize door, I found Mr. Thanos near it. He stood still, peering toward the front of the house and the wide hall where I assumed Lord Alfred had met his demise.

The floor was polished walnut, dark with a fine sheen, no rug to mar its surface. The front door led into a foyer, which had another door between it and the main hall. The foyer's door, with stained glass in its upper half, stood open, though the front door was now closed.

The hall flowed past one large set of closed double doors, which I assumed led to the drawing room. The staircase came next, rising gracefully to the next floor. Opposite the staircase was another set of doors. One of these was open, giving me a glimpse of the dining room, which was still filled with people in fine clothes. The gentlemen wore black suits and sharp white cravats, while the ladies were in gowns of light spring colors.

The inhabitants were extraordinarily silent, though I saw one gentleman pouring brandy at the sideboard. I presumed none of them knew exactly what to do.

Of Albert's body, there was no sign. Nor did I see any blood staining the perfection of the floor.

Mr. Thanos too wore a black suit, though his cravat was

crooked and one of his waistcoat buttons had come undone. I was used to seeing him in plainer suits of flannel or wool, but black broadcloth suited his slim figure, dark hair, and soft brown eyes.

"Mr. Thanos?"

At the sound of my voice, Mr. Thanos jumped, his feet nearly coming off the floor before he spun to face me.

"Oh, Mrs. Holloway." He pressed a hand to his heart. "You startled me."

I gestured to the front hall. "Is that where …?" I whispered the question, not wanting Mrs. Bywater, who I caught sight of in the dining room, to realize I was upstairs.

Mr. Thanos nodded. "Gave me quite a jolt to rush out here and see the poor chap crumpled to the floor. He'd greeted me in the drawing room not a half hour ago, and he was breezy and trying to be witty, though he said his stomach was troubling him. Stabbed, the housekeeper said. Front door was wide open. They've moved him into the drawing room." He waved a hand at the closed doors.

"No one was stationed in the foyer?" Usually, in fine houses, a footman was assigned to stand at the front door so they could help guests from carriages and usher them inside. They also safeguarded the house from any would-be intruders.

"No, no, Lady Babcock had all the footmen in the dining room serving. Too many guests for her number of staff, Cyn mused to me in a whisper."

"The front door was left unlocked while no one was there to stand guard?" I asked in wonderment.

"I suppose." Mr. Thanos blinked. "I really have no idea."

"I see no blood," I remarked. Not that I wanted to gaze upon such a thing, but it was strange.

"Yes, I noticed that. He was lying on a rug, which the three footmen lifted and carried into the drawing room with Lord Alfred on it. He's still in there, stretched across the sofa."

Which meant Alfred hadn't bled enough for it to seep through the rug to the boards beneath.

Mr. Thanos drew a breath. "Such a shock. Truth to tell, I am glad you have popped out, Mrs. Holloway. I meant to tell you, I discovered what was in the teacup. There were barely enough dregs to make a study, but one of my chums at the Polytechnic is a clever chap. He could isolate the various components of air itself if he could put it into a beaker. And I believe he can. You have to—"

"What was in the tea, Mr. Thanos?" Sometimes rudely interrupting Mr. Thanos was the only way to gain information.

"Eh? Oh, yes. I beg your pardon. It wasn't laudanum. It was morphine."

He gazed at me in triumph, but I was no more enlightened.

"Morphine?" I repeated dubiously. "I've heard of it. It's a sort of medicine, isn't it?"

"Yes, it can alleviate pain, but too much is quite deadly. Mixing it with alcohol or something like laudanum will speed up its effects, but one can die in a few minutes from having even a small dose."

Cold flashed through me. "A mercy I only had a swallow, then."

His eyes widened. "You drank some? Good heavens, yes, it is a mercy. Also, the tea diluted it a good bit, according to my friend. I am happy to see you alive and well, Mrs. Holloway."

My knees were shaky, and I put my hand on the wall to steady myself. "Thank you for finding out, Mr. Thanos."

"Not at all. Are you well?" He regarded me with concern in his kindly dark eyes.

"Yes, I will be." I hadn't drunk more of the tea, and I was quite fine, after all. No need to break down.

The question remained, who had dosed the tea for Mrs. Morgan and why? Had her initial illness been true, or also caused by a dollop of morphine?

I drew a breath, remembering my errand. "Come downstairs with me. Lady Cynthia is there, and I know you haven't had enough to eat."

Mr. Thanos gave me another concerned glance but followed me to the backstairs door, reaching to open it for me before I could. He could not help always being the gentleman, even to a cook.

By the time we reached the kitchen, Tess had returned. "I told him," she whispered to me as I began to fix Mr. Thanos a plate. "He sent me back here and hurried off."

I nodded at her in thanks and carried Mr. Thanos's meal to him.

He rubbed his hands. "Seems callous to want food at a time like this, but thank you, Mrs. Holloway."

"I said the same thing," Cynthia stated. She and Mr. Thanos shared a tiny smile of camaraderie, which pleased me beneath my bewilderment.

I agreed with Jane that a tramp swarming into a fine home on Portman Square and stabbing the young master to death as he happened to cross the hall was an unlikely occurrence. Constables walked their beats in these parts, even on Easter Sunday, and one would be certain to notice a vagrant looking for unlocked doors.

The idea came to me that perhaps the open door was a blind, and someone already in the house had decided to do away with the young master. One of the guests enraged with him? A servant, such as Armitage, who might strike out in a drunken stupor if Lord Alfred argued with him?

I would more believe it the work of an intruder, if it weren't for Mrs. Morgan. She'd been afraid for some reason, and the tea intended for her had been laced with poison. Had Lady Babcock wanted Mrs. Morgan sunk into a long stupor or perhaps out of the way entirely?

Mrs. Seabrook had mentioned that Mrs. Morgan and Lady Babcock had been quarreling "something fierce," speculating it was over the menus. But Lord Alfred's death cast a more sinister shadow on the arguments. Had Mrs. Morgan realized that Lady Babcock meant to do away with her stepson? Tried to persuade her against it? Therefore, Mrs. Morgan had to be taken out of the way?

Then again, I reasoned, Lady Babcock might not have tampered with Mrs. Morgan's tea at all. If she'd set the cup down somewhere between wherever she'd brewed it and the cook's bedchamber, anyone could have slipped the poison into it.

Anyone in the house at the time, I amended. Which meant the servants and the rest of the family.

I had no idea how difficult it was to get hold of morphine. Was it something only a doctor could dispense, or did one walk into the nearest chemist's shop and request it? Mrs. Seabrook had mentioned that a doctor did give Lady Babcock medicine, but she hadn't specified what.

These were questions the police would have to ask, as it was not my place, but the two events narrowed down the list of suspects.

Then again, the incidents might be entirely unconnected. Lady Babcock, in her rather dim way, might have been trying to nurse Mrs. Morgan back to health, and had nothing to do with whoever had killed Lord Alfred.

Watch out for her, Mrs. Morgan had urged me.

Because she thought the woman might kill her stepson?

I needed to know who had been in or outside of the dining room when Lord Alfred had died.

Under the pretense of packing up the food, I moved to the table near Cynthia and Mr. Thanos so I could have a low-voiced conversation with them.

"Who were the guests today?" I asked Cynthia.

Her light blue eyes went wide. "Good Lord, are you thinking one of them killed Alfie while we were enjoying our soup?"

"It is one possibility," I said cautiously.

"Well, let me see." Cynthia's eyes narrowed in thought. "There's Margaret, of course, Alfie's sister. Another member of the family turned up—Desmond Charlton. Third cousin, I believe. Margaret is batty about him. Wants to marry the fellow, though Lady Babcock doesn't approve of the match. Desmond and his brother haven't much money, at least, not enough for Desmond to marry Margaret and keep her in the manner to which she is accustomed. Then there was a bishop, whose name I can't remember—"

"Norris," Mr. Thanos supplied.

"Norris," Cynthia repeated. "A few friends Margaret invited that I know fairly well myself—Catherine and Thomas Bowler, who have recently made a match. Alice Hodgkinson and her sister Caroline, who are of eligible age, probably brought to entice Alfred to propose to one of them. Their brother Cuthbert, who was likely there as a potential husband for Margaret. As I say, Lady Babcock doesn't like Margaret's attachment to Third Cousin Desmond, so she's always matchmaking for Margaret. Auntie and Uncle, of course. Thanos. Me. Oh, and Lady Babcock's aunt, whose name I also can't remember."

"Miss Jordan," Mr. Thanos said.

"That's it. Jordan. She faded into the woodwork, as though she didn't want anyone to notice her. Not that I blame her. Both Margaret and Alfred were rather rude to her."

Mrs. Seabrook had referred to Miss Jordan scoffingly as a nobody. I imagined the son and daughter of the house thought the same, especially as they didn't seem pleased with their stepmother.

Her ladyship ain't wanted, Mrs. Morgan had said about Lady Babcock. *No one can stick her.*

I wondered why Lady Babcock had invited her aunt when she herself wasn't welcome in her own husband's house. But perhaps Miss Jordan hadn't had anywhere else to go for Easter. Perhaps the woman thought it better to suffer some rudeness in exchange for an excellent dinner than to sit alone at home.

I myself would rather fix a simple meal and enjoy my own company, but others did not have such fortitude. And perhaps Miss Jordan didn't have the means for even a simple meal. The upper classes were full of impoverished and forgotten gentlewomen.

"All remained in the dining room?" I asked as I laid Mr. Davis's unopened wine bottles into their crates. "For the first part of the meal?"

"Once we were being served, yes," Cynthia answered. "Before that, we rather drifted about. Foul-tasting ratafia in the drawing room, though I longed for a stiff whiskey. Then we wandered from there to the dining room, no gentlemen taking in the ladies or anything like that. Very informal, and rather haphazard, which is how Lady Babcock prefers things. My aunt had much to say about that, but I like Lady Babcock. An uncomplicated woman."

"Any of us could have lingered to stab Lord Alfred, I suppose," Mr. Thanos said. "I can't say who exactly was in the dining room at any one time except myself and Cynthia, of course, before the soup was served." He blenched. "What a horrible thought. No, it *must* have been an intruder, don't you think?"

Mr. Thanos's words and expression pleaded with me to agree. Much easier to believe an anonymous person of the streets had broken into the house and done murder, than someone one had sat down to a meal with.

"I find it odd that the front door was left unlocked and unbolted when there was no footman to guard it," I said.

"Exactly," Cynthia agreed. "Very likely it wasn't unlocked at all, and the murderer opened it to make it seem so. Which means, Thanos, it must have been one of the dining party, I'm sorry to say. The bishop is a shifty cove, I've always thought."

I could not tell whether she'd have believed such a thing if Alfred hadn't been murdered. But then, not all members of the clergy were upright beings. Some were given livings based solely on their connections rather than any religious leanings.

"I also find it odd that Lord Babcock wants it kept quiet," I said. "Lord Alfred is his son and heir. Shouldn't he want to know who murdered him?"

"Yes, but what a scandal if it's known Alfie was killed in

his own house," Cynthia answered. "They'll never live it down. I'll wager Lord Babcock will put about that Alfie died of sudden illness and swear us to secrecy."

"Or, his lordship already knows who killed him." I firmly set a lid onto the box of wine. "And wants to spare that person the gallows." Would he stand by his own wife, I wondered. If she'd murdered his beloved son?

"You don't suppose Lord Babcock killed Alfie himself?" Cynthia's brows rose. "That can't be, can it? What man would kill his own son?"

"'Cause maybe he ain't his son." Jane had paused in her duties to listen, and now she dropped this interesting bit into the conversation.

"Why on earth would you say that?" I demanded. I ought to admonish Jane for eavesdropping, interrupting, and stating such slander, but I was too curious to be very outraged.

"The first Lady Babcock had many beaus, so they say," Jane said without compunction. "Wasn't pure as the driven snow when she married his lordship. I've heard it was put about that his young lordship wasn't actually the marquess's son."

"That's not true," Mary flashed, also having drifted to us. "He's a fine young man—" She broke off, tears filling her eyes, as though she realized she now had to speak of Lord Alfred in the past tense.

"Oh, he's the son of an aristo, all right, but which one?" Jane said darkly. "Begging your pardon, your ladyship."

"Never mind … Jane, is it?" Cynthia said. "I've heard that rumor myself, but I think it's all rot. Alfie resembles—resembled—Lord Babcock quite a bit, so no one officially questioned Alfie's legitimacy. The first Lady Babcock took that secret to her grave, if it was even true, so we shall never know."

"It is of no matter anymore," I pointed out gently. "Who will inherit Lord Babcock's title now? Third Cousin Desmond?"

Cynthia shook her head as she chewed a mouthful of ham and aspic. "Desmond's older brother, Stephan. He's not here today, as he is in France for reasons that are not clear. Desmond is representing their branch of the family. With Alfie out of the way, Stephan is the heir, Desmond the spare." She coughed and reached for the glass of wine I'd poured for her. "I say, you don't mean that *Stephan* did it? Disguised himself as a tramp and all that and stabbed Alfie? To clear the way for their twig of the family tree?"

"Anything is possible," I said with a shrug.

As I'd learned through helping Daniel investigate crimes, the police were usually less concerned with *why* a person was killed than proving who had done it. There was plenty of motivation for murder—a person might be a wealthy man who would bequeath a large sum when dead, or he'd aggravated the wrong person too many times, or he was the victim of a robbery or some other random crime.

In Lord Alfred's case, he stood in the way of another man inheriting a title and an estate. Illegitimate children could not inherit, of course, no matter what, but if no one *knew* Lord Alfred was illegitimate, or no one could prove it—or if it wasn't true at all—then there wasn't much any doubters could do. But perhaps there was enough shame or fear of the truth that someone in the family had decided to make the question irrelevant. Now this Stephan would inherit, and his brother had been conveniently in the house.

Or perhaps Lord Alfred had simply angered someone,

who'd struck out in rage, whether they'd meant to kill him or not.

How they'd managed to kill the man while everyone had been in sight of each other in the dining room was another problem.

Not that I would have the chance to look into the matter. This was not my kitchen or my house. I was being bundled back to Mount Street as unceremoniously as I'd been bundled to Portman Square.

Armitage put an end to our conversation by storming rather unsteadily into the kitchen.

"Are you still here?" he demanded of me. "You'd better clear out right quick, Mrs. Cook. The police have arrived, and they're questioning everyone in the house, like the bastards they are."

*H*aving delivered his message, Armitage stamped down the passageway to his butler's pantry and slammed the door.

Jane's face went tight. "The police? I can't have no dealings with the police."

Why not? I wondered. Guilty conscience? And about what?

"I will not let them question you without me by your side," I promised her.

I'd learned from experience that constables or sergeants weren't always kind to servants, often assuming one of them was the culprit from the outset. Any reported theft or murder in a home led police directly to the staff. With the entire dinner party in the dining room digging into the fish, that left any servant wandering the house as a suspect.

Which included Mrs. Seabrook, I reminded myself. She'd claimed to be tidying up the drawing room and heard the front door open. She could have quietly stabbed Lord Alfred, opening the door to hint at an intruder.

Despite Lord Babcock's wishes, the police were here now. Tess had reported to Daniel, who'd have gone straight to Scotland Yard. We'd watched from the stairs outside the scullery while men in severe suits carried out Lord Alfred's body on a draped stretcher and loaded it into a van, presumably to take to a morgue. Mary had renewed her weeping as they went.

Lord Babcock had walked out with his son. He was a tall man, but his frame was bowed with grief. He rested a hand on the stretcher before the bearers loaded it, as though saying good-bye.

My eyes filled with tears as I watched. Poor man.

I had hoped that Inspector McGregor would be called upon to run the investigation. Though he disliked my interference, he'd believe me if I told him the kitchen staff had been with me working hard while the crime had been committed.

I heard McGregor's rumbling tones outside as we returned to the kitchen, but it wasn't he who descended below stairs to interview the staff. It was Sergeant Scott.

I'd first met Detective Sergeant Scott when he'd detained Lady Cynthia's father last fall in connection with a murder. The sergeant was a tall, youngish man with a sharp face, fair hair slicked against his skull, and shrewd blue eyes that took in everything around him.

If the sergeant was surprised to encounter me in this house, he made absolutely no sign of it. He instructed me to send in the kitchen servants to speak to him one at a time in the housekeeper's parlor before walking purposefully there and closing the door.

Cynthia and Mr. Thanos had retreated upstairs after Armitage's announcement, as they would be interviewed as well. They'd sent me sympathetic glances as they went but could no longer help me.

I decided to approach Sergeant Scott first. I entered the housekeeper's parlor to find a small room containing a few comfortable chairs, a writing desk, and a sideboard with a half-full carafe of wine reposing on it.

Sergeant Scott had pulled the desk away from the wall so he could face his suspects and had set a chair in front of it for those he'd interrogate. He did not look up when I entered, only continued scribbling into a small notebook.

I declined the silently offered chair, preferring to stay on my feet. "Is Inspector McGregor speaking to the upstairs?" I asked before Sergeant Scott could address me. "He should be told that the footmen were instructed to be in the dining room, leaving the front door unguarded, which is a strange thing to do. Inspector McGregor might be wise to find out who gave the order."

Sergeant Scott continued writing for a moment, though whether he took note of my observation or ignored it, I couldn't say.

He at last fixed me with his pale blue gaze. "Mrs. Holloway, you are cook for a family in Mount Street, not this house."

No question of whether I'd changed my place of employment since I'd seen him last. He knew I didn't work here and waited for me to explain my presence.

"Lady Babcock's cook has taken ill. Mrs. Bywater volunteered my services."

His brows rose slightly. "Do you often cook for other households on your mistress's whim?"

"No," I said, a bit too quickly. "This was an unusual circumstance."

Sergeant Scott's pencil scratched on his page. "The nature of the cook's illness?"

"I don't really know. She is poorly, I can tell you that. The morphine given her can't help, can it?"

The pencil abruptly ceased. Sergeant Scott looked up at me again, his eyes even sharper. "What morphine?"

"It was introduced into her tea. I have no idea who put it there."

"How do you know she was given morphine? And that it was in the tea?" His skewering gaze told me the most likely answer was that I'd put it there myself.

"Because I accidentally drank it," I admitted. "Fortunately, only a small mouthful, but the effect was strong, and the tea was terribly bitter. I gave the cup to Mr. McAdam to test. The report I received was that there were trace amounts of morphine. I am not certain if the dose was meant to murder the cook, make her ill, or make her well. The lady of the house carried it to her, but that does not mean she put the morphine in it."

"You knew poison had been put into a cup of tea, and you didn't summon a constable?" Scott demanded.

In my younger days, I might have wilted before his accusing stare, but I'd grown strong. "I did inform the police, in a way. I gave the cup to Mr. McAdam. As I say, the morphine might have been put there for benevolent reasons. If Mr. McAdam had been alarmed, he'd have told Inspector McGregor."

"McAdam doesn't answer to McGregor," Sergeant Scott growled.

"I know," I replied as calmly as I could.

Daniel worked for a horrible man called Monaghan, but I had no idea how much Sergeant Scott discerned of the exact nature of Daniel's assignments. I knew very little myself, because Daniel wasn't allowed to tell me. Scott knew *something* of it, but it wasn't for me to babble about Daniel and the tasks Monaghan set him onto.

Sergeant Scott regarded me severely for a few more seconds, then returned to his book. "Describe the events of today, leading to the death of Lord Alfred Charlton."

"We were busy preparing the Easter dinner," I said. "Which is quite a long process. None of us left the kitchen, that I saw, once all the guests had arrived. Hours pass quickly when one is cooking, and it is a miracle we finish it all by the time the butler summons the diners. We had ham and its accompaniments, a mutton shank and some quail, all the vegetables, the fish and the soup, bread to go with every course, not to mention the pastries and tarts I'd been working on over the past week—"

"Given that you were paying close attention to your tasks," the sergeant interrupted me. "Could it be that you didn't notice anyone from downstairs nipping up to the main floors? Lord Alfred was fatally stabbed in the base of his neck. Death would have been very quick, and the murderer back in place before she was missed. You likely have a number of deadly knives in the kitchen. My constable is even now collecting them."

I briefly reflected that it was a mercy I'd decided against bringing my own. "Why did you say *she*?" I asked. "You suppose the murderer was a woman?"

"All the male servants were in the dining room, according to the butler," Sergeant Scott answered without hesitation. "That leaves the female servants unaccounted for."

"You wouldn't be so certain of the killer's gender if an

intruder walked in and did it," I pointed out. "You are assuming someone in the house killed Lord Alfred?"

"I assume nothing, Mrs. Holloway. I only note what happened so the inspector will have as much information as possible to make an arrest."

His words were logical, but I was not reassured. "Lord Alfred was wandering the house, I've been told. He might have met his death *before* everyone was settled in the dining room, if one of the guests lingered to speak to him. You say it would have been very quick—how do you know he wasn't dead before the meal was served?"

Sergeant Scott's next glance told me he found me irritating and arrogant. "I will speak to the rest of the kitchen maids," he said, ignoring my question. "Their names?"

I bristled at his preemptory tone but answered without argument. "Tess Parsons, who is my assistant. Jane, the undercook, and Mary, scullery maid. I don't know their surnames, but Mrs. Seabrook will." As Sergeant Scott wrote this down, I continued, "I will remain while you question them. They're fearful, which is understandable."

"No, I will speak to them alone, without them looking to you for instruction on how to answer."

"I'll not abandon them, Sergeant," I said tightly.

Sergeant Scott frowned at me but remained cool. "You will not be—"

He broke off on a sudden, staring sharply at the door. I heard what he did, the sound of bottles clinking.

Scott rose and swiftly stepped past me. He wrenched open the door to reveal Armitage staggering into the hall with a large crate of wine bottles.

"You there," the sergeant demanded. "What are you doing?"

Armitage started, nearly dropping the box, but an answer sprang readily from his lips. "Moving the master's wine to a safe place. If there's a tramp lurking about, I need to make sure he don't nick anything, don't I?"

He lied—a few of those bottles were ones I'd brought that I hadn't finished packing. Armitage's safe place was likely one in which he'd either drink all the wine or sell it on.

Sergeant Scott detected the lie as well. "Put them down," he ordered.

"*I* didn't kill the young master. You're no one to tell me what to do—"

"*Now.*"

Armitage started again but after assessing the sergeant's impatience, he lowered the box to the slate floor. He straightened, one hand going to his back.

"*You* can answer to the master if they go missing," Armitage muttered both to me and the sergeant. "And put them all back. I have me duties to attend."

"I will speak to you soon," Sergeant Scott informed him. "Wait in there." He pointed to the butler's pantry.

Armitage began to splutter, but again, he wilted under Scott's cold stare. Armitage sent me a baleful glance but scuttled into the butler's pantry and slammed its door.

I moved around Sergeant Scott to peer into the box. "Half of those belong to the Mount Street house," I said. "May I take them?"

Sergeant Scott studied me without expression. I knew he did not give two sticks about who the wine belonged to, but he also knew that aristocrats were possessive of their expensive wine collections. He gave me a minute nod.

"Send in Miss Parsons when you go."

Without giving me a chance to answer, he stepped back

into the housekeeper's parlor and closed the door with a decided click.

I'd never heft six bottles of wine under my arms, so I began to shove the crate down the hall toward the kitchen. I half expected Armitage to pop out and accuse me of theft, but he stayed put. Sergeant Scott, without ever raising his voice, had thoroughly intimidated him.

I was not as worried about Tess facing Sergeant Scott alone, despite some petty thieving in her past, because she'd grown less fearful about the police in the last few years. Her beau, Caleb Greene, was a constable, and she'd helped Daniel and me in some of our investigations. Tess had finally concluded that the Peelers were simply men doing a job, though there still were plenty of constables who thought nothing of bullying innocents.

I entered the kitchen half bent over the box I was pushing.

"You are next, Tess," I said breathlessly, and then added for the benefit of the others, "Sergeant Scott can be aloof, but there's nothing to be frightened of. Just tell the truth. We were all here in the kitchen when the young master died."

I heard no response, so I straightened up, pushing tendrils of hair from my face. Tess and Mary regarded me with worry.

"I'm not afraid," Tess said. "But Jane's gone."

"Gone?" I shoved at another recalcitrant tendril. "What do you mean *gone*?"

"She legged it," Mary supplied. "Not ten seconds after you went into the room with Old Bill. She tore away her apron, and off she went."

CHAPTER 8

I uttered a few choice words under my breath as the other two watched me in trepidation.

Jane fleeing might have nothing to do with Lord Alfred's death, I told myself. The theory went that a guiltless person had no reason to run from the police, but I knew that in reality, plenty of people who'd done no wrong had been banged up, myself included. The instinct to take to one's heels was understandable.

Even so, it would be far better for Jane to stay and face Sergeant Scott than give him an excuse to arrest her.

"Tess, take our wine out of this crate and put it with what we brought," I said. "Then go down the hall and speak to Sergeant Scott. Mary, carry on with what you were doing, and under no circumstances allow Mr. Armitage to come in here and abscond with more bottles. I will find Jane."

So speaking, I removed my apron, snatched up my hat, and charged out of the house, taking the outside steps as rapidly as I could.

It was a bright, sunny Easter afternoon, perfect for families who lived on the square to stroll in Portman Square's small park, as many now did. Children smiled at mothers and fathers, who put aside their aristocratic arrogance to teach games to their sons and daughters, nannies hovering to ensure their charges were on their best behavior.

No one bothered to take note of a woman in cook's garb rushing along the street, searching every which way for an errant kitchen maid.

If Jane knew London well, she could be far away by now, gone to ground as only born-and-bred Londoners could. We might never see her again.

I doubted very much that Jane had stabbed Lord Alfred, but Sergeant Scott or Inspector McGregor might decide to arrest her in absentia and send out constables to scour the streets for her.

I headed down Orchard Street, reasoning that Jane would flee east and south as quickly as possible. She might have family or friends in that part of the metropolis or across the river who would take her in.

Long before I reached Oxford Street, I found Jane.

Or rather, I saw her struggling hard against Daniel, who was still dressed in his shabby clothes and trying to hold on to her.

I neared them just as Jane gave Daniel a hearty kick in the shin. Daniel winced, but his grip did not loosen.

"Stop," I commanded Jane.

She swung to me, her eyes wild. "Mrs. Holloway, help me get away from 'im. 'E's a madman."

"No, he is not. He is a friend, and you need to cease."

Jane's surprise stilled her. "A friend?" She studied Daniel in distaste. "What sort of friends you got, Missus?"

"Very good ones," I said. "Why are you trying to run, Jane?

The sergeant will immediately suspect you're guilty, when I know you are not."

"Course I ain't. Who says I am? I never stuck a knife in the young master. Why should I? I keep myself well away from the likes of *'im*."

"Exactly," I said. "You were in view of me the whole time today, which I have already told Sergeant Scott. But taking flight will not help. Why did you run?"

Jane began to struggle again, but this was futile against Daniel's strength. "Make 'im turn me loose," she wailed.

"I think I'll hang on to you a bit," Daniel replied cheerfully.

Jane glared at me. "Are you a procuress? And here I thought you was pure as the driven snow."

"Certainly not." My tone was stern. "I am neither of those things."

"Then why won't you let me go? It ain't your business, and I can be well away."

"If the sergeant and inspector take it into their heads that you're guilty, they'll hunt for you across London and not stop until they find you," I said. "You'll never work again, and you'll endanger any family or friends you run to."

Jane stilled, as though she hadn't considered this. That she hesitated to endanger loved ones raised her in my estimation.

"Tell *me*, at least, why you ran," I went on. "We'll decide what the sergeant needs to know."

Jane's eyes widened. "You wouldn't peach?"

"That rather depends. Have you been pinching things from the house?"

"No." Her quick outrage made me believe her. "I ain't a fool. I'd get the noose for that."

"Then why?"

Jane went quiet in Daniel's grip, though he was experienced enough not to release her. "I think her ladyship killed him," Jane said mournfully. "Only, I don't blame her, like. His young lordship was always so awful to her. I don't want to say nuffink that will get her into trouble."

I listened in surprise. I hadn't thought Jane an admirer of Lady Babcock, though when I thought it through, she'd been more dismissive of Lord Babcock and his first wife. It had been Mrs. Morgan who'd told me the second Lady Babcock had been no better than a tart, and Mary who'd derided her.

"Why do you say this?" I asked Jane. "Except for the fact that Lord Alfred was rude to his stepmother, there must be another reason you suppose it."

Jane cast a sidelong glance at Daniel. "Is this the Mr. McAdam you were talking about? The one you sent Tess out to find this morning?"

That she'd deduced this made my respect for her rise even more.

"At your service," Daniel said in his most congenial tone. "You can tell us anything, Jane. We're good at keeping things confidential."

"You talk funny for a tramp," Jane declared, then she heaved a resigned sigh. "All right, I'll tell you. Her ladyship and Cook have been arguing back and forth all week, going into corners and speaking sharply, arms waving. I caught sight of her ladyship with Mrs. Morgan in the larder, and her ladyship *never* comes below stairs. Mrs. Morgan went upstairs a time or two as well, which ain't usual. I expected Mrs. Morgan to get the sack any day, but then she grows powerful sick. And now ..." Jane's voice grew thick with tears. "I ain't staying in a house where the family murders each other and poisons the staff."

I could not argue this last point. "If you believe her ladyship did these things, why do you not want to tell the police?"

"'Cause she's been kind to me, hasn't she?" Jane turned to me pleadingly. "She made old Seabrook hire me, when I didn't have nowhere to go. Her ladyship caught me shivering on the street steps and told me to go into the kitchen, eat something, and then help out a while. That were about a year ago—I been here ever since. Seabrook tells us not to speak poorly of her ladyship, but she don't like her, that's certain. I had to pretend I felt the same, in spite of her ladyship's charity to me, so I could keep on Seabrook's good side." She sagged. "I try not to talk about her at all."

An interesting tale. It sounded as though Lady Babcock indeed had a kind heart beneath her vacant expression. Even if Lady Babcock had not, in fact, laced the tea with morphine, she'd been concerned enough about her cook, despite their quarrels, to look in on her.

I was impressed that Lady Babcock had retained her compassion after she'd been thrust into her husband's family and lived for years surrounded by people who didn't like her.

Would a person who took pity on a girl in the street murder her husband's beloved son? As far as I knew, Lady Babcock had no children, so she wouldn't be clearing Lord Alfred out of the way so her own son could inherit. She also didn't sound like a lady who would lash out in a pique.

"It seems unlikely Lady Babcock stabbed him," I told Jane. "She and Mrs. Morgan could have been arguing about what to serve for Easter dinner, which has nothing to do with the murder."

I didn't quite believe that, but I needed to reassure Jane.

"Suppose," she conceded.

"Sergeant Scott only wishes to know where you were when the murder occurred. You were helping me in the kitchen. Tess and I had eyes on you the entire time. That is all you need to tell him."

"Mary nipped out for a bit," Jane said unhappily.

I came alert, as did Daniel. "Pardon?" I asked.

"After we sent up the fish and were in a bother about getting the ham and its fixings ready at the same time. I saw Mary slip out the back door and go up the outside stairs."

Had she? I'd never noticed, but we'd been focused on the meal, and Mary had been elbow-deep in her sink, or so I'd believed.

"She was back down when Mrs. Seabrook announced his lordship's death," I recalled.

Mary had been more outraged than the rest of us when Mrs. Seabrook had told us the meal was off. Had Mary already known *why* it was, her reaction feigned?

Mary had professed great admiration for Lord Alfred. Had she been madly in love with the young man? If he'd rebuffed her, and she'd been upset … Oh, dear heavens.

"I will speak with Mary," I said firmly. "Jane, you go back inside, tell Sergeant Scott when he calls for you exactly where you were before Lord Alfred was found, and remain silent about everything else."

"I know how to keep mum," Jane declared. "I only told you, because you and your man pried it out of me. I was afraid the Peeler would too."

"You've confessed it to us, so your conscious is clear. Now, return before Sergeant Scott decides you've run away and sends constables out to find you."

Jane nodded, as though agreeing to be sensible. Daniel finally let her go, and she walked away from us, squaring her shoulders as she went.

I kept a sharp eye on her, but she made for Portman Square without breaking stride. I'd be right behind her as soon as I finished speaking with Daniel.

I turned to him, my resolve cracking. "Please tell me Lord Alfred had so many enemies that anyone in London could have broken in and killed him in his own front hall. I don't like to think someone who lives in the house did it, even though I know it's most likely."

"He seems to have been a well-liked young man about Town." Daniel dashed my hopes for an easy solution. "His father, on the other hand, is a stern taskmaster and has made many political enemies. It is possible one of them decided to rid him of his heir to take their vengeance, but improbable they'd do it in such a haphazard way."

"Lord Babcock wouldn't invite his enemies to dine in his home with his family, would he?" I mused. "Lady Cynthia described the guests, who seem innocuous enough. Though I suppose one never knows."

"Unfortunately, true." Daniel scanned the street, as though watching for any observers. "Cheer up. The police might conclude that someone in passing realized the front door was unguarded, entered to rob the place, encountered Lord Alfred in the hall, stabbed him, and fled. It is plausible."

I also preferred that solution, but something in my bones told me it wasn't true. "If the police dismiss the murder as a burglary gone wrong, when it wasn't, then others in the house might be in danger. Lady Babcock herself."

I pondered anew Mrs. Morgan's admonition to me about Lady Babcock. *Watch out for her.*

Instead of a warning against the lady, could it have been a plea? *Watch out for those trying to harm her.* I truly needed to speak to Mrs. Morgan again.

"Daniel, when you were worried about me going to Portman Square, why?" I asked abruptly. "Did you believe something bad would happen at that house?"

"No." The word was spoken forthrightly. "I'd have done everything in my power to prevent you entering Lord Babcock's abode if I'd thought a murder would occur there. But, as you've no doubt concluded, I've had business in this square before. One of Lord Babcock's neighbors knows who I really am. Well, one of my personas while working for Monaghan, I mean."

Daniel finished wistfully. *Who I really am.* He didn't know, not for certain.

I wanted to take Daniel into my arms there and then and tell him it didn't matter. He was himself, and that was enough for me.

However, we stood on a public street near the happy families of Portman Square, with me in my work dress and Daniel garbed as an unsavory vagabond.

"Is that why you are in your current guise?" I asked. "Instead of off having Easter dinner with your son?"

Daniel huffed a laugh. "I couldn't watch over you if Lord Babcock's neighbor recognized me as the rather annoying secretary he'd employed last year. Also, James is lurking too, but he's better than me at being unobserved. He insisted on helping." His expression held forbearance.

"Oh." I darted my gaze about but saw no one who resembled the tall James. "Well, tell him he has become quite skilled."

"Nothing that should worry a father," Daniel said tightly.

James was a good lad, I knew. He'd take care of himself, and Daniel too.

"Speaking of fathers," I continued. "Do you know if there is any truth to the rumor that Lord Alfred wasn't Lord Babcock's son?"

Daniel shook his head. "Probably not. From what I understand, Lord Babcock and his first wife were a devoted couple. The first Lady Babcock bore Lord Alfred several years into the marriage, so he cannot have been the product of a liaison before their engagement. I believe the first Lady Babcock gained her reputation for promiscuity because she had many offers to wed in her youth. She turned them all down to choose Lord Babcock, who was fifteen years her senior and a respectable marquess to boot. The younger gentlemen were jealously enraged, the young ladies who'd hoped to land themselves a lordship were furious, and so the rumors began."

"Despicable," I said in disgust. "Because the woman found someone she liked better than the twits who fluttered about her?" I'd seen similar young bucks flirt determinedly with Cynthia because her father had a title, as well as young lady debutants sneer at her for being unmarried still.

I tamped down my outrage to return to our problem. "How do you know all this?" I asked Daniel. "Do you have a dossier on every family in Mayfair?"

"The neighbor. When I was with him in my capacity as a snobbish secretary, he gossiped at length about everyone he knew."

Daniel would have tucked away these bits and pieces of information in case they came in handy with an investigation later. That, and he was simply interested in people.

I reluctantly stepped away from Daniel, resigning myself

to the reality of the day. "Well, I must return and make certain Jane speaks to the inspector, and then visit Mrs. Morgan."

Daniel put a hand on my arm. "Take care," he said in a low voice. "Someone in that house is not averse to sliding a knife into whomever they wish. I'd rather you and Tess returned home and let McGregor and Sergeant Scott handle things."

"I will, once the person is arrested and taken away," I promised. "I don't like to leave Jane and Mary to the machinations of the police."

"You have no obligation to either of those young women," Daniel pointed out.

"Why does that matter? If there is danger in Lord Babcock's home, I can't callously abandon them to it."

Daniel's smile told me he liked my answer. "I will be nearby, if you need to shout for me. As I say, so is James."

"I will be careful, I promise you." I should turn away now and hurry back to the house, but I hesitated. "I wish ..."

"Yes?" Daniel asked with interest. "What do you wish, Kat?"

His voice had grown quieter, and the space between us decreased.

What I wished was to go home with him, to have the only Easter dinner I cooked be one for him, James, and Grace. To have my own life instead of dedicating all my time to those who little appreciated it.

I let out a breath. "Never mind. No use pining for castles in the air."

Daniel's hands closed around mine and squeezed them. I thought he would speak, give me hope for such a future, but in the end, he only flashed me his warm smile, released me, and faded into the shadow of the fence.

I made myself turn and leave him, squaring my shoulders as Jane had done, and walked back to the house in Portman Square.

———

I WANTED TO SPEAK TO MARY FIRST THING UPON MY RETURN and question her about leaving her post, but I did not see Mary at her sink.

"She's in with the sergeant," Tess informed me. "Jane's next."

Jane was busily spooning cooked vegetables into bowls to be covered with cheesecloth and stored in the larder for later consumption. She glanced up at me when Tess spoke her name but remained silent. She looked more at ease, though, and I hoped I'd reassured her somewhat.

For now, I prepared several pots of tea and a large platter of pastries I'd meant for the Easter dinner. The ladies of the house would be upset with the arrival of the police, and tea and pastries might soothe them. I made a smaller pot and plate for Mrs. Morgan and asked Tess to help me carry it all upstairs.

Before we could leave, Mary banged out of the house-keeper's parlor and dashed into the kitchen, tears smeared on her face.

"I never," she sobbed. "I never killed him. I loved him. *Tell* him, Mrs. Holloway."

CHAPTER 9

$\mathcal{I}$ stepped out of the kitchen to find Sergeant Scott at the door of the housekeeper's parlor, a look of resignation on his face. He made no move to pursue Mary or make an arrest.

"Send in the other kitchen maid," the sergeant instructed me, then disappeared back into the room.

Jane, her face wan, quietly moved around me and down the hall. She rapped once on the door, then entered, her body stiff.

I returned to the kitchen once Jane was safely inside. I knew Sergeant Scott would not let me in there with her, and I only hoped my admonition to be sensible and say little helped her.

"Sit down, Mary," I told the weeping girl. I fetched another teacup, poured the hot beverage into it, and set the cup on the table next to her. "You were wrong to run upstairs when we were so busy, but you did, and there's no use breaking down over it. If Sergeant Scott believed you'd gone up to murder the young master, he'd have arrested you on the spot."

"I didn't," Mary wailed. "I just wanted to catch sight of him, like."

"Of course you did." I remained firm but put some sympathy in my tone. "The important point, Mary, is whether you saw anyone else when you were hoping for a glimpse of Lord Alfred."

"I never did see him." Mary sniffled. "Saw everyone else milling about, drifting to the dining room, but not his young lordship."

"When you say *everyone else*, who do you mean, exactly?"

"His sister and stepmum, with their stepmum's aunt." Mary pulled a handkerchief from her pocket and swiped at her nose. "His dad and cousin. Your ladyship friend and her beau. They took their time going in, chattering to one another as they wandered down the hall. The rest was already in the dining room. Mrs. Seabrook was there too, clearing up the drawing room behind them. I was ever so afraid she'd see me."

"What about Lord Alfred?" I asked. "Had he gone into the dining room? Or back into the drawing room? Perhaps he spoke with Mrs. Seabrook?"

Mary shook her head vehemently. "I told you, I never saw him. Don't know where he was."

This was interesting. If Lord Alfred hadn't been with either the group in the dining room or those in the hall, where had he been? And why?

"Did you tell Sergeant Scott this?" I asked.

Mary nodded. "He made me go over it and over it, but I know he thought I did it." Her sobs renewed.

I had not imagined the weariness in Sergeant Scott's expression when he'd watched Mary run to the kitchen. Her histrionics must have worn down even his stoicism.

"Have a cake and drink that tea," I ordered. "You will feel better. Then continue putting away the food. Tess, help me with the trays."

My crisp instructions cut through Mary's weeping. She nodded and obediently lifted the teacup to her lips.

Tess rolled her eyes behind Mary's back but seized the heaviest tray and moved off toward the backstairs. I picked up the second tray and followed her.

When we reached the main floor, we found the house very quiet. The dining room and drawing room doors were both closed, Inspector McGregor presumably interviewing the guests behind one of them.

I asked a footman, who was now diligently watching the front door, where the ladies of the household were. He regarded me sullenly and pointed upward with a stiff finger. I sent him a sharp frown then bade Tess continue up the main stairs.

The large first floor held only a sitting room and a library, so on we went to the next floor, where the mistress's boudoir was likely to be. A maid who was nipping from bedroom to bedroom, linens in her hands, guided us to Lady Babcock's chamber.

"Thank you," I said to the maid.

She paused to whisper to me. "The breakfast you cooked for us was ever so nice. Wish you could stay here."

I nodded at her compliment, though all I wanted to do after this day was return to my familiar demesne of Mount Street.

The maid opened the door for us, and Tess and I strode inside with our burdens.

Lady Cynthia rose from a settee she shared with the young woman I assumed was Lady Margaret, the deceased's man's sister. Lady Babcock sat on a chair at her dressing table, removed from them, wearing a bewildered expression.

An older woman with a thin face and graying hair reposed on a delicate chair in the corner near the window, as though not wanting to be noticed. I deduced she was Miss Jordan, Lady Babcock's aunt.

Miss Jordan flashed a look at me as I entered that told me she saw more than her passive way of carrying herself indicated.

Mrs. Bywater, fortunately, was absent. She was not the sort of person one wanted close when needing comfort.

"I brought a repast, your ladyship," I said when no one spoke.

I set the smaller tray on a table near the door and moved to help Tess with the large one, which we placed on the low table in front of the settee. Cynthia seated herself again and immediately began dispensing tea, as neither Lady Babcock nor Lady Margaret seemed able to take on the task.

Lady Margaret's eyes were red-rimmed, her face blotchy. I noted that she smelled strongly of a floral perfume, possibly donned to entice her cousin Desmond, or perhaps it was something she wore for supper every day. Lady Cynthia never wore scent, not liking to smell like a chemist's shop, she always jested.

"I don't want anything," Lady Margaret declared tearfully. "Take it all away."

"Nonsense." Cynthia finished pouring a cup and shoved it

at Lady Margaret. "Best thing for shock is to take nourishment. Else you'll waste away."

As Lady Margaret possessed the artificial slenderness so popular these days, it wouldn't take much for her to fade to nothing.

Lady Magaret grasped the teacup and saucer, either because she agreed with Cynthia or because Cynthia was a stubborn force.

I pushed the plate of pastries toward them. I'd worked hard on these, laminating the dough and brushing some with jam, others with chocolate and hazelnut cream.

Cynthia took up a jam pastry and bit off a large chunk while Lady Margaret regarded them listlessly.

"Perfect," Cynthia stated after she chewed and swallowed. "Mrs. Holloway has a fine touch."

I nodded my thanks as I fixed a cup of tea and carried it to Lady Babcock. "I've put a bit of sugar in this and a dollop of cream," I told her as I held it out to her. "It will fortify you nicely."

Lady Babcock took the cup, gazing at me as though she'd never seen me or anyone else in the room before. Of the three ladies, she seemed the most dazed.

"What has happened in my house?" Lady Babcock murmured to me, so softly I barely caught it.

I bent closer. "Lord Alfred's death is a terrible thing, your ladyship, I know. We can only let ourselves grieve and then carry on."

This is what I'd told myself after my mother had died. The words sounded as hollow now as they had then. I'd been fortunate to have Joanna to hug me until my weeping ceased, and not much longer after that, I'd borne Grace. Grace had done much to return happiness to my life.

"They don't want me to carry on," Lady Babcock said to me, *sotto voce*. "They want me to hang for murdering Alfred."

I could not say, *Of course, they don't*, because it had been made clear that most in this household did not want her here.

Would Lord Babcock's lofty position protect Lady Babcock if she was accused? I dimly recalled some law or other from the past that said a husband was responsible for his wife's wrongdoings, but I wasn't certain if that was still the case.

The law might, at the very least, have Lady Babcock put into an asylum for the insane—one of those remote country places with thick walls and strong gates. Lady Margaret and the servants might be pleased by that outcome.

The question was, would any of them go so far as to sacrifice Lord Alfred to rid themselves of Lady Babcock? The idea seemed far-fetched. It was more likely that Lady Babcock's enemies would take advantage of the situation to try to pin the crime on her.

That left the problem of who had actually crept up behind Lord Alfred and stabbed him.

"All will be well," I said softly to Lady Babcock. "Drink your tea."

She lifted the cup to her lips and took a long swallow. That she did so without hesitation, made me believe she hadn't, in fact, dosed Mrs. Morgan's tea. Lady Babcock would be more suspicious of a cup I handed her if she was used to manipulating people with dollops of morphine.

Once Lady Babcock seemed calmer, I carried tea to Miss Jordan. She took it with murmured thanks.

"Will you look out for her?" I whispered.

"Of course," Miss Jordan said stoutly.

A dragon, I decided. One in simple gray broadcloth.

Would *she* have killed the son of the house to protect Lady Babcock from him? Perhaps Lord Alfred had gone beyond rudeness and had dealt the occasional blow to his disliked stepmother—it was not unheard of. Miss Jordan might have decided he needed to be taken from Lady Babcock's life. An idea worth pondering.

Miss Jordan began sipping her tea, ignoring me, and I returned to the others. Tess had quietly served Lady Margaret some of the cakes, though the young woman only stared at the plate on the table.

I signaled to Tess that we should leave. Tess curtsied to the room, eyes down, as though she was the most obedient maid in the history of maids. I lifted the tray I'd prepared for Mrs. Morgan, and Tess followed me out.

"Whew, I don't envy our Lady Cynthia staying in there," Tess murmured to me as we reached the door to the back stairs.

"Neither do I," I agreed as Tess opened the door for me. "Back to the kitchen for you, Tess. And thank you. On a cheerful note, we should be home soon."

"That's the truth." Tess grinned at me and then clattered down the stairs while I ascended them.

I found Mrs. Morgan sitting up in her bed, looking much better. She'd obviously drunk no more morphine-laced tea today.

"Ever so kind," Mrs. Morgan said as I laid the tray on her bedside table. "What with all the goings-on here, I think I'll give me notice."

"Perhaps that would be for the best." I poured out a cup of tea, added a bit of sugar, and handed it to her.

Mrs. Morgan's eyes narrowed, though she readily took the cup. "Are you after my post, Mrs. Holloway?"

"No, indeed." I'd have to be desperate to work for this family, I decided. "I only meant you might be happier elsewhere."

"Could be. Course, if I leave, her ladyship will be thrown to the wolves."

"You are afraid *for* her." I'd finally settled on that interpretation of what she'd been trying to tell me before.

Mrs. Morgan took a noisy sip of tea. "Even her own husband can't be bothered with her most of the time. Besotted at first, because she was once so lovely, but she don't have much in the way of good sense. A man gets weary of that, don't he?"

It occurred to me that in his time of loss, Lord Babcock hadn't wanted his wife next to him. He might have ordered her to withdraw to her chamber with Lady Margaret and Cynthia, or perhaps it had been Cynthia's suggestion.

"I don't believe she killed Lord Alfred," I said.

"Eh? Of course she didn't. Her ladyship don't have that sort of cunning. I tried to tell her to be careful in this house, what with how the family treats her, especially with young Desmond arriving."

Third Cousin Desmond, whom Cynthia had told me about. "Would Cousin Desmond risk murdering Lord Alfred?" I wondered out loud. "His brother, Stephan, is the one who will inherit." So Cynthia had indicated. "Does he dote on his brother so much that he'd sacrifice himself to ensure Stephan is the next marquess?"

Mrs. Morgan snorted a laugh. "Not young Desmond, that scrawny nuisance. I've known him since he was in short pants, and believe me, he has no love for his older brother.

No, if he offed Lord Alfred, it would be in a fit of pique alone. Young Alfred used to poke fun at him something awful, and young Desmond was always a bit sensitive."

"Lady Margaret wants to marry him?" I'd have thought the pampered young woman I'd observed downstairs would prefer a handsome, brawny, and very wealthy man to be her husband. Wouldn't hurt if he was already a duke or some such.

"Those two have been thick as thieves since they were children. Lady Babcock believes Lady Margaret ought to marry a quiet man and go live in the country somewhere, instead of larking about the metropolis with her friends. Girls these days are bold as brass, ain't they?"

Lady Margaret had seemed more lethargic than bold, but then, she'd suffered a shock from the loss of her brother this day. Her face had betrayed her weeping. Perhaps she ought to marry Desmond after all and try to find some happiness.

"Mark my words," Mrs. Morgan went on darkly. "It were Seabrook what killed him, if it were anyone."

I started. "Why do you say that?"

Mrs. Morgan shrugged. "She never liked Lord Alfred. Lord Alfred always ragged on her, just as he did to his stepmother. Lord Alfred was a cruel young man to his own family. Outside it, butter wouldn't melt in his mouth, as they say. Had much of polite society wrapped around his finger."

I'd already wondered whether Mrs. Seabrook, upstairs in the drawing room once the diners had departed it, had done the deed, for whatever reason. She was a robust woman.

Other ideas poured through my head, distracting me as I nodded at Mrs. Morgan. "No doubt the police will find the culprit."

"Those fools? Ha. Couldn't find a piece of hay in a

haystack." Mrs. Morgan slurped her tea noisily and reached for the pastry.

"I'll leave you to it," I said, as Mrs. Morgan had fixed her attention on her repast. "I'm sure your kitchen maids will be happy to have you back again."

Another snort told me what Mrs. Morgan thought of my platitudes.

I departed as she masticated the pastry, and descended once more below stairs.

———

By the time I reached the kitchen, Tess and Mary had made good headway on packing up our things. Jane was less downcast though still tense.

"The sergeant were ever so polite," Jane told me, sounding reluctant to admit it. "It was like you said, Mrs. H. He only wanted to know where I was at half past one, when we was sending the meal upstairs. He didn't want me to tell him anything else."

I did not know Sergeant Scott well, but he seemed to me a practical man. He wouldn't be interested in Jane's past if it wasn't relevant. The sergeant could be as intimidating as the growling and grumbling Inspector McGregor, though in a cool way I found a bit more frightening than the inspector's bluster. However, Sergeant Scott had proved his pragmatism in my last encounter with him.

As we continued the work, I heard a familiar click of heels in the passageway, heralding the arrival of Mrs. Bywater. She gazed about the room when she arrived, focusing on the foodstuffs still waiting to be put into their crates.

"Leave nothing behind," she admonished me. "All these

vegetables, all these potatoes. They should already have been packed."

"Not those." I shielded a basket of leftover produce. "I purchased them for *this* house."

"Did you?" Mrs. Bywater widened her eyes. "Then they come with us. Lord Rankin will reimburse you through your wages."

"I put them on the marquess's account, ma'am." I bobbed a shallow curtsey as though I was in awe of saying the word *marquess*.

"Oh, well, in that case." Mrs. Bywater backed away from the argument. "Be sure to pack what is ours, including what you've already cooked. We can dine on that for a few days. And all of the wine. Close up those crates, Tess, before someone takes anything."

Mrs. Bywater shot a quick glance at Mary and Jane, as though certain they'd pinch the leftovers and rush out into the street with them. Mary regarded her fearfully, Jane with a scowl.

"All our things will go back to Mount Street, I assure you," I said in soothing tones.

"See that they do. I'll visit the larder this evening and check, so no giving things away or eating them yourselves."

"Of course, ma'am." I gave her another curtsey.

Mrs. Bywater's eyes narrowed at my sudden docility, but she changed the subject.

"Leave out a loaf of bread and some butter," she instructed me. "So that Lady Babcock and her husband will have something to eat. I adore Lady Babcock—so generous to our little charitable society—but she is apt to forget simple things like nourishing herself."

I had the feeling that if the family wished to eat at all, they'd need more sustenance than bread and butter.

"Is his lordship all right?" I asked Mrs. Bywater. "Considering."

"Lord Babcock is made of stern stuff," Mrs. Bywater said decidedly. "He still has an heir, so all is not lost."

Jane blinked at this callous statement, but she quickly dropped her gaze and helped Tess nail the crates shut.

Mrs. Bywater winced as Tess gave her crate a hard blow with a hammer. Mrs. Bywater sniffed, looked over the kitchen once more, and thankfully took herself away.

"I was right," Jane said once we heard Mrs. Bywater retreat and the backstairs door slam. "She *is* a cow."

"Enough," I told her, but gently. "I will run out and see if we have a cart to tote this home in."

I headed up the stairs, not bothering with a coat. The spring day had become even warmer, and I perspired as I hurried to the road where I'd last seen Daniel. I hoped he'd lend his delivery wagon, as no other was in sight. Apparently, Mrs. Bywater hadn't thought through how we'd lug all these things back.

Daniel was no longer at the railings where I'd left him. As I paused, contemplating where he might have gone, James spoke behind me.

"He's gone."

I spun around, my hand to my heart. "Good heavens, James. You do like to spring from nowhere."

"Sorry, Mrs. H.," James shot me a lopsided grin that was so like his father's. "Dad went off to assist Inspector McGregor. The inspector's decided to arrest the murdered man's cousin for doing the deed, and the cousin is cutting up rough."

"Third Cousin Desmond?" I asked in astonishment. "No, that is all wrong."

I hadn't heard any shouting or seen Inspector McGregor bundling Cousin Desmond out into the street, but we'd been hastening to pack under Mrs. Bywater's admonishments, Tess enjoying making a racket with the hammer.

James shrugged. "Right or wrong, they're hauling him to the magistrate. Dad had to help the constables hold on to him. They're trundling him off, even as we speak."

CHAPTER 10

"Third Cousin Desmond did not kill Lord Alfred," I declared.

"Do you want to run after them?" James asked. "Tell Inspector McGregor?"

I nearly did let myself chase whatever police wagon had taken away Cousin Desmond, but I stopped. Neither Inspector McGregor nor a magistrate would be interested in my thoughts at this moment, and I had no evidence that could clear Cousin Desmon's name. My idea that he couldn't have done it would be dismissed.

No, sensitive Desmond might have to spend a night in Bow Street or even Newgate, though Lord Babcock, if he could, would prevent that.

Desmond was now second in line for the marquessate. If he disliked his older brother as much as Mrs. Morgan said he did, he might not, in theory, stop at anything to become the marquess himself. A magistrate and a high court judge might believe that.

"No," I said. "I will have to do this another way. Any

chance your dad's delivery wagon is about? I must trundle all our goods back to Mount Street. The sooner, the better, I think."

James touched his cap. "Right away, Mrs. H."

He sprang away with the enthusiasm of youth, leaving me pondering as I walked back to the Babcock house.

The news of Desmond's arrest had reached the kitchen by the time I arrived.

"I never liked him," Mary said darkly. "He was always cruel to the young master. Calling him a bastard, and all."

Mrs. Morgan had said the opposite, that Lord Alfred had taunted Third Cousin Demond. I couldn't be certain which was the truth. A bit of both, I supposed.

If Cousin Desmond had believed the tale that Lord Alfred was illegitimate, that might make Desmond's motive to kill Lord Alfred even stronger in the eyes of the law. Lord Babcock had apparently been satisfied that Alfred had sprung from his seed, but rumor was a powerful thing.

Tess and I had nearly finished bundling away our things —I had no leisure to sit in a corner and ruminate—when Lady Cynthia entered the kitchen.

"Can you take another pot of tea to Margaret?" she asked. "She is beside herself now that her beloved Desmond's been arrested so quickly after she lost her brother."

Lady Cynthia spoke briskly, as though she was becoming rather fed up with the traumatic events in this house. She obviously pitied Lady Margaret, however. Hence the order of tea.

"Of course," I said. "Tell her not to worry. I don't believe her cousin did it."

Cynthia studied me in relief. "I'm happy to hear you say

that. Margaret doesn't need more trouble. I don't think Desmond did it either. He's a bit of a weed."

"Perhaps you ought to go home now," I told her kindly. "There's not much more you can do."

"I'd love to, but I'll stay on." Cynthia heaved a resigned sigh. "McGregor dismissed the other guests, who have all fled. Lord Babcock has shut himself into his study, not wanting to see anyone but his valet. Auntie is already storming home. Apparently, she is annoyed she was in a house where a murder was committed and has no intention of staying any longer."

As Mrs. Bywater could be trying on her best days, I thought perhaps it was better for Lord Babcock's family if she went.

"I'll have the tea ready in a trice and bring it up," I told Cynthia, then leaned to whisper to her. "Make certain no one eats or drinks anything I haven't prepared, and eat nothing that has been left unattended for even a moment."

Cynthia's eyes went wide. "Do you think the poisoner will strike again? Do they mean to kill everyone in the house?"

"We can sincerely hope not. But please monitor the food and drink after I'm gone."

"That I will. Good Lord."

"Thank you." I returned to my usual tones. "Have you seen Mrs. Seabrook at all?" The housekeeper had been notably absent since announcing Lord Alfred's death.

"She's rushing about, clucking, because the upstairs rooms have been left in such a state. She's busy chivvying the maids to put them to rights."

I imagined Mrs. Seabrook gave orders like a general in battle. "Up you go. I'll bring the tray."

"You are too good for us, Mrs. H."

I accepted the compliment with modesty, as usual. Cynthia grinned at me then took herself away.

James thumped down the outside stairs and knocked on the door to announce the cart was ready. Tess brightened when she saw him, and Jane and Mary did as well, though for different reasons. The kitchen maids were no doubt noting that James was quite handsome.

"My, my," Mary said after James had hefted a few crates outside. "Ain't he a one?"

Her tone was admiring, which told me her attachment to Lord Alfred had been little more than a passing infatuation.

Jane said nothing at all, but the way her gaze fixed on James showed genuine interest. James was a free spirit, I wanted to tell them, not ready to walk out with a young lady, but I held my tongue. Let them have this one refreshing moment in a bleak day.

While Tess continued to supervise the packing, I prepared a fresh pot of tea, added pastries that would not survive the journey back to Mount Street, and once more ascended through the house. When I paused on the first floor, I saw Mrs. Seabrook issuing stentorian commands to two maids who rushed about, trying to obey her.

Lady Babcock, Miss Jordan, Cynthia, and Lady Magaret had remained in Lady Babcock's chamber.

Lady Margaret was crying fresh tears, wiping them copiously on an already wet handkerchief. Her eyes were redder than before, and she morosely regarded the tea I set before her.

When I carried tea to Lady Babcock, she gazed up at me with more resolution than she'd had when I'd left her.

"I've made up my mind," she said quietly. "I'm going to

live with my aunt for a bit. She needs looking after, and I will welcome the change."

"Perhaps that is the best thing, your ladyship," I agreed.

I was not horrified or disapproving that she'd abandon her husband while he grieved for his son. If Lord Babcock had wanted her comfort, she'd already be shut in the study with him.

I had the feeling I was witnessing the shattering of a marriage. The Babcocks might not shock the world with a divorce, but I wagered they'd begin living separate lives. It was too bad, but I'd experienced a difficult marriage myself, and being on one's own was infinitely preferable to that.

Cynthia encouraged Lady Margaret to sip some tea. Margaret coughed as it went down, but she managed to swallow then fell limply against the settee's pillows once more.

I sent Cynthia an inquiring glance, wondering if she needed me to stay, but Cynthia nodded for me to go.

I hoped she'd persuade Lady Margaret to bed and to take something to make her sleep, though not the morphine that was floating about this house. I wondered if Sergeant Scott would search for it, or if he and Inspector McGregor would be satisfied that they'd caught the killer and not bother.

Desmond couldn't possibly have laced Mrs. Morgan's tea, I was certain. He hadn't arrived at the house until shortly before dinner was served today.

Why Mrs. Morgan's tea had been dosed was still a mystery. Had Mrs. Morgan guessed that Lord Alfred would be murdered, and the murderer wanted to shut her up? But if so, Mrs. Morgan could have passed that information on, either to me when I'd taken her the broth, or later, when she'd felt better.

The effect of Mrs. Morgan's illness was that she hadn't been in the kitchen. The morphine might have been intended to make certain she stayed abed.

Had the person thought to poison Lord Alfred and blame the kitchen staff, or whoever took over for Mrs. Morgan, for serving him bad food? Was Mrs. Morgan the sort of cook who'd never let anyone near her dishes?

If so, the poisoner must have been dismayed at my diligence. I too let no one near the food except those I trusted, and as I'd told Mrs. Seabrook, I tasted everything myself.

Was that why they'd risked stabbing Lord Alfred?

In any case, Third Cousin Desmond had not been here to dollop morphine into Mrs. Morgan's tea.

That left Mrs. Seabrook, Lady Babcock, Lord Babcock, Lady Margaret, Alfred himself, Armitage, and the maids and footmen. I'd think only a physician would be able to get hold of morphine, but I acknowledged that anything could be stolen from anywhere.

I gave Lady Babcock and Miss Jordan one last glance of reassurance and left the room, breathing a sigh of relief when I closed the door behind me. Cynthia would guard the ladies well. I told myself there would be no more murder or attempted murder if we all remained diligent.

By the time I reached the kitchen once more, James and the three maids had finished loading the cart. I snatched up my coat and hat and ascended the outside stairs to find Tess climbing to the seat next to James for the ride home.

Mary leaned on the railings, gazing at James, her expression forlorn.

Jane faced me belligerently. "If ye had any heart, ye wouldn't go."

I regarded her with surprise. "My dear Jane, this house

already has a cook. I cannot remain where I'm not employed."

"Then take me with ya."

I felt sorry for her, but there was little I could offer. "Hiring another kitchen assistant is not up to me," I said gently. "But I can put in a word for you at my agency if you wish to seek a better place."

Jane considered this, then softened. "That'd be good of you. Thank you, Mrs. Holloway."

"Not at all. Now, look in on Mrs. Morgan and make sure she gets well. Also, if Lady Cynthia asks you to help prepare food or drink this afternoon and evening, do your best to assist her."

Jane looked mystified at this request, but she nodded. The next moment, she amazed me by throwing her arms around me. "I'm so glad you came."

I returned her embrace, giving her an affectionate squeeze. "I'm glad I have as well."

Jane released me and self-consciously brushed tears from her eyes.

I definitely would request that my agency find Jane a much better place. She was skilled in the kitchen and shouldn't be held back. If I hadn't already had Tess, I'd have tried to persuade Mrs. Bywater to hire her.

As it was, I knew Mrs. Bywater would never agree to the expense of a second kitchen assistant, even if Lord Rankin was paying the bills. She'd have to write to Lord Rankin and explain, and I knew she feared annoying the titled man she was related to only through the marriage of her niece.

James gave us a cheery wave and started the cart down the street. Tess also waved her good-byes, the two maids returning them downheartedly.

As on the journey here, there was no room for me on the cart, so I chose to walk home. I bade the two maids farewell, vowing to look in on them from time to time. Jane nodded, but Mary burst into tears again as I turned away.

Once I crossed Oxford Street, I exhaled in relief. I saw James in his cart turn ahead of me, and I slowed my steps. I was in no hurry to unload the goods and then prepare the Bywaters a thrown-together supper to make up for their missed Easter feast. I was tired and out of sorts on this thoroughly rotten day.

James had pulled the cart to a halt in front of the house by the time I reached Mount Street, and Tess was scrambling to the ground. Without a word, James descended and started lugging the heaviest crates down into the kitchen. The lad was a blessing.

Mr. Davis waited for us below stairs, anxiously supervising James as he toted in the wine.

"I hope it hasn't been shaken up too much," Mr. Davis said worriedly. "Will ruin it, that will."

"We have been very careful," I told him as I hung up my coat and hat. "Do count and make certain they are all there, Mr. Davis, except for the two I used for sauces. The butler to Lord Babcock tried to abscond with some."

Mr. Davis's mouth pinched. "Armitage, you mean. He's a nasty piece of work. Has nicked things in great houses the length and breadth of England. I will count with double care." Mr. Davis waved me off. "Thank you for bringing the wine back, though in what state, remains to be seen."

"Not at all, Mr. Davis."

I left him brooding over the bottles like a doting father and turned to assist Tess and Elsie, who'd left her scullery, to put everything away. Tess told Elsie what that had gone on in the Babcock household, Elsie listening with rounded eyes. Mr. Davis and Mrs. Redfern, as well as the footmen, paused to listen, but I silently got on with preparing supper for the family.

I reflected on it all as I worked, shutting out the voices around me.

I could not make the pieces of the puzzle fit, and that annoyed me. The poisoning and the stabbing, regardless of what I'd speculated earlier, may or may not be connected. The antipathy for Lady Babcock, the question of Lord Alfred's legitimacy, Lord Babcock withdrawing to his study, and Mrs. Morgan's warnings might all be smoke.

However, as Inspector McGregor constantly pointed out to me, it was the business of the police to investigate and decide if they had enough evidence to charge someone with murder. In truth, none of this had anything to do with me.

And yet, I couldn't help wanting to protect the people in that house: Lady Babcock, who was out of her depth; Jane and Mary, who were innocent young women; Mrs. Morgan, who wasn't a bad sort; Lady Margaret in her intense grief. Even the brusque Mrs. Seabrook had my concern. She certainly could have committed both crimes, though I wasn't sure what she would gain by it.

I did consider that Mrs. Morgan herself could have done the murder. She could have dosed her own tea with an amount of morphine that wouldn't kill her in order to feign an illness, waited until the family and guests had gone into dinner, nipped down the backstairs, stabbed Lord Alfred, and scuttled again to her bed.

As in the case with Mrs. Seabrook, *why* Mrs. Morgan would do such a thing, I had no idea, although she'd proved to be as protective of Lady Babcock as Lady Babcock's aunt professed to be.

Of course, this idea would suppose Mrs. Morgan knew about morphine and how much to use on herself. Plus, she'd have to be swift, something her age and bulk might prohibit. In addition, she'd have to know that Lord Albert would linger in the hall after the others went into the dining room. He'd claimed an aching stomach—which could mean he too had been given something to make him hesitate instead of hurrying in with the others to eat a large meal.

I continued to speculate as we finished unpacking the foodstuffs and preparing the meal for the Bywaters, but I drew no definite conclusions. Mrs. Bywater did indeed visit the larder after supper, and she seemed disappointed she couldn't find fault with how I'd stored the leftovers.

Once she went upstairs again, we and the rest of the staff consumed our own suppers, and Tess, Elsie, and I cleaned up the subsequent mess.

I sent Tess to bed before long, as she was exhausted after our two extraordinary days. I remained in the kitchen after last of the staff had gone up, sitting at my familiar table and making notes in my book.

My hopes were that Daniel would come. I'd put aside some cold ham and a leftover bit of tart for him, but I had no idea if he'd have time to visit me. He might be assisting Inspector McGregor to determine whether Desmond had murdered his cousin Alfred.

I continued to write well past midnight, making scribbles in the margins when my thoughts wouldn't connect.

I realized after a while that I'd drawn a flower several times over. I halted my hand in surprise and stared down at it.

Of course, I thought, but I followed that with the words, *Make certain.*

I closed the notebook and rose, quietly moving down the passageway to the housekeeper's parlor. I had a key to it and unlocked the door.

The shelf in the corner held my three cookbooks. I flipped through one of them until I found its section on herbs and spices. I read the page I sought, my heart speeding.

I replaced the book on the shelf and returned to the kitchen in time to hear Daniel's knock on the back door. I quickly opened it, pulling him inside and embracing him with relief.

Daniel no longer wore an indigent person's garb but his own coat, homespun trousers, and thick cotton shirt. He also smelled nice, of the outdoors and coal smoke, nothing like the miasma that had clung to him with his disguise.

He returned my hug, pressing a kiss to my cheek. "That glad to see me, are you?"

I made myself release him. "I am always pleased to see you, Daniel, though I know you've only come for your Easter meal." Before he could answer my teasing, I drew him all the way inside and shut the door against the night.

"Let us sit and have tea," I said, towing him to the table. "And I will tell you who killed Lord Alfred."

*D*aniel regarded me with a satisfying amount of surprise, his hand poised on the back of a chair. "You know?"

"I believe so," I amended. "Do sit down, please. Your hovering makes me nervous."

Daniel scraped the chair back and dropped into it obediently. "Do you plan to report your conclusions to Inspector McGregor?"

"I am reporting to *you*. I might be wrong, and I'd like your opinion before you make it known to Sergeant Scott or Inspector McGregor."

"I am agog to learn your solution." Daniel spoke lightly, but his expression held tension.

I took some time brewing tea and fetching the ham and rolls from the larder while Daniel watched me intently.

"That the police think it was done with a knife from the kitchen is interesting," I began as I sat next to Daniel and laid a fork and napkin near his plate. "It means the culprit had access to the kitchen, or to someone in the kitchen who could fetch the weapon for them. That person also would have to somehow obtain morphine."

Daniel lifted his fork. "You believe one person did both?"

"Yes, and I know why, although I don't know precisely how. Nor do I know the exact sequence of events. I can only guess them."

Daniel smiled as he scooped up a bite of ham. "Your guesses in the past have proved more accurate than those of the most thorough detectives I know."

"Very flattering," I admonished but good-naturedly.

I poured out the tea and proceeded to tell him all.

———

"THE LADIES WILL BE DOWN DIRECTLY," LADY CYNTHIA SAID TO me the next morning as she admitted me to the dining room of the Portman Square house.

I wasn't comfortable speaking to the family in the upstairs rooms, but Cynthia had wisely pointed out that Lady Babcock, Lady Margaret, and the marquess would be even more uncomfortable below stairs.

I could not, in good conscience, sit in an aristocrat's drawing room as though I were an honored guest—though I wore my best frock and hat, not my kitchen garb—but I acceded to the dining room as neutral territory. What I cooked ended up there, after all.

Mrs. Morgan was back in her kitchen, I learned upon arrival, but she'd given her notice. So had Jane. In the meantime, Jane carried in a tray of tea things and a platter of cakes to nourish us.

Jane curtsied deferentially to Cynthia, gave me a nod with the hint of a smile, and disappeared again.

The gilded clock on the sideboard ticked monotonously a few more minutes before Mrs. Seabrook led the two ladies of the house into the room. Mrs. Seabrook wouldn't look at me, but her movements were stiff with disapproval. She likely blamed me for the cook and Jane giving notice, and she'd be correct.

Lady Margaret, dressed in a black silk gown that didn't fit her well—possibly quickly altered from something borrowed —kept her head bowed. Her unhappiness rolled from her, touching me palpably. She plunked herself in the chair at the foot of the table and gazed unseeingly out of the window.

Lady Babcock's dark frock, by contrast, had clearly been tailored for her, likely leftover from the last person she'd mourned. The cut had been in fashion only a few years ago, which meant her loss had been recent. My pity for her increased.

Cynthia poured tea for all as they got settled. Lady Babcock sat in a chair halfway along the table. Miss Jordan, still in the plain gray broadcloth frock I'd seen her in the day before, planted herself firmly in a chair by the sideboard, which put her almost directly behind Lady Babcock. The dragon was guarding her well.

Lord Babcock was the last to arrive. This was the first time I'd seen the man close to. He was tall and gaunt, his graying hair and lined face betraying his age. He also dressed in mourning, and his withdrawn manner touched my heart. It was obvious he had been grieving deeply. Whatever rumor surrounded Lord Alfred's origins, this man had cherished his son.

The way Lady Babcock followed her husband with her gaze as he passed her without a word told me she was still in love with Lord Babcock, despite his seeming indifference.

I wondered if Lady Babcock truly would go live with Miss Jordan for a bit, and what affect that would have on Lord Babcock.

"Thank you for coming down," Lady Cynthia said to the ladies and Lord Babcock as he took his place at the head of the table. "Mrs. Holloway had some news this morning. Your cousin Desmond will soon be released."

The reactions around the table were varied. Lord Babcock's thick brows shot upward, he clearly curious how a cook of all people would know such a thing, but I caught relief in his eyes.

A pucker appeared between Lady Babcock's brows, and Miss Jordan, if anything, looked angry.

Lady Margaret's reaction was the most dramatic of all. She burst into tears and collapsed forward onto the table. "Thank God," came her muffled words. "Thank God."

Mrs. Seabrook pulled smelling salts out of her pocket and hurried to Lady Margaret. Before she could reach the young woman, Lady Margaret sat up and wiped her eyes with an embroidered handkerchief. Mrs. Seabrook stepped back but kept the salts at the ready.

"Of course, he is not guilty," Lady Margaret declared, her voice hoarse with weeping. "Never was. Didn't I tell you?"

"You did tell me," Lord Babcock rumbled gently. "Do not give way to hysteria, my dear. *You.*" His gentleness fell away as he pinned a stern gaze on me. "What do you mean by coming here and upsetting us? Why should the police tell *you* anything about our cousin?"

I had remained standing, knowing better than to sit at a table with an aristocrat and his family. I gave him a deferential curtsey. "I have friends who work for the police, your lordship. They decided the news would be best coming from Lady Cynthia and myself."

Lady Babcock raised her chin, her gaze alert. "Quite right," she said in her soft voice. "We've had enough of police in the house."

Miss Jordan agreed with a nod, though she said nothing. No one else in the room paid any attention to her.

Lady Margaret also did not speak, but her glance of intense dislike toward her stepmother told me she hoped the culprit would be Lady Babcock. How satisfying for her to watch Lady Babcock be shoved into a police wagon and taken away forever.

"I'll have Mrs. Holloway explain," Cynthia said. "She can relay it clearly. But I must say that I agree with the solution and so does Inspector McGregor. He will be along soon."

Lady Babcock's eyes widened. "Good heavens. Do you mean the killer is still here?" She sent a fearful gaze to the closed double door, as though the murderer would leap through it, brandishing a knife.

"Of course it is what she means," Lord Babcock snapped at her, his eyes holding both rage and worry. "Carry on, Mrs. Holloway." His tone told me that I had better make his attendance at this tableau worth his while.

"Your ladyship," I said, speaking directly to Lady Babcock. "Has someone prescribed for you a packet of morphine powder? Or perhaps a liquid dose?"

Lady Babcock started. "Yes, indeed. My doctor. For my nerves. He told me to take only tiny bits at a time."

"Mrs. Morgan's dose was more than a tiny bit," I said. "It was enough to kill someone if they took the entire dollop. Thank heavens Mrs. Morgan did not." And *I* did not, I added to myself.

Mrs. Seabrook scowled at me. "Do you mean to accuse her ladyship of trying to poison Cook? You are highly impertinent, Mrs. Holloway."

"Not at all," I said quickly. "I am only pointing out that there was morphine in the house. Anyone who knew of it could have taken some to either harm the cook or at least lay her up for a while."

"Why should they?" Lord Babcock demanded.

It was quite unnerving for me to face Lord and Lady Babcock and tell them of the goings-on in their household. If Lord Babcock chose to be offended, he could have a word with Lord Rankin, and I might be out of a place in an instant. He could also spread the word to his cronies to tell their wives not to hire me.

I curled my fingers into my palms and forced myself to continue. They deserved the truth. And who knew who else might die before the killer's wild scheme was concluded?

"Mrs. Morgan suspected that there was danger in this house," I told him. "I don't believe she knew exactly what would happen, but she knew *something* was wrong. She tried to warn Lady Babcock, but Lady Babcock did not want to believe her. These are the arguments the kitchen staff and Mrs. Seabrook witnessed. Mrs. Morgan confirmed this to me when I arrived today."

Lady Babcock gave me a faint nod. "She was right. I ought to have listened."

"At some point during the week, when Mrs. Morgan began to feel unwell—likely already being given the morphine—and the kitchen maids were preoccupied trying to carry on without her, the killer took the opportunity to pinch the kitchen knife that did the murder."

Miss Jordan made a soft sound of surprise, that again, no one else noticed.

Lady Margaret turned her gaze to her stepmother, waiting for me to denounce her. "How awful."

"All of you had access to the kitchen," I went on. "Mrs. Seabrook included, of course. It stands to reason, as this is your house. Lady Margaret went down from time to time to consult on dishes or to snatch a bite between meals, and lately, Lady Babcock went to continue her discussions with Mrs. Morgan. The only one who did not habitually go below stairs is your lordship."

Lord Babcock nodded once. "No reason for me to."

"The kitchen is a woman's domain, for the most part," I said. I did know some masterful male chefs, and I'd worked in a house where the husband had enjoyed cooking an omelet when he felt peckish, but in general my statement was correct.

"Her ladyship did come down quite often this past week," Mrs. Seabrook said in hushed tones.

"Mrs. Morgan is very protective of you, your ladyship." I gave Lady Babcock a polite nod. "It is good of her. She nearly died for that protection."

"What are you telling us?" Lord Babcock demanded. "That someone wanted to kill our cook as well as my son?"

His voice cracked on the last word, and I sent him a glance of sympathy. "Yes. I do not know if Mrs. Morgan suspected exactly what would happen, but the killer couldn't take the risk. If Mrs. Morgan grew ill or died, sickness or bad food could be blamed. She would also be out of the way for the Easter meal, which was when there would be opportunity to strike. With so many people in the house and the confusion between drawing room and dining room, there would be a chance to corner Lord Alfred alone. Perhaps he was also made to feel unwell so that he'd not rush in to dinner with the others. The open door could suggest an intruder, but if the police saw through that ruse, there would be plenty of other people in the house at the time who could be suspected. To Lady Margaret's regret, Mr. Desmond Charlton, of whom she is fond, was blamed."

Lady Margaret did not like me saying her name, but the corners of her lips softened. "At least dear Des has been proved innocent."

"It ought to have occurred to you that in the eyes of Detective Inspector McGregor, your cousin Desmond would have the strongest motive," I said. "He is now closer to inheriting the title and your father's wealth." I looked directly at Lady Margaret. "If you do marry Mr. Charlton, my lady, I will worry about the health of his older brother."

I heard intakes of breath around the room, and Lady Margaret stilled. "I beg your pardon? Are you accusing *me*?" She rose stiffly from her chair, her glare intense. "I'll have you sacked for implying such a thing, perhaps even arrested. Papa, do something about her."

"Let her speak." Lord Babcock's strong voice cut through his daughter's. Lady Margaret gaped at him, but she sank into her chair again, her cheeks scarlet.

I cleared my throat. "There is a flower—jasmine—that grows in warm climates but is cultivated in this country in hothouses. The blossoms are lovely and fragrant. Unfortunately for some people, they can cause a bad reaction, mostly itchy skin, and red, watery eyes. A person with this sensitivity could rub their face on the plant and make it appear as though they'd been weeping heavily."

"I *have* been weeping," Lady Margaret declared. "Why should I not be? My brother is dead and my beloved cousin was taken to the magistrate for it. I *do* have an arrangement of flowers in my bedchamber, which might include jasmine, but I am not sensitive to it at all."

"Yes, you are," Lord Babcock broke in. "Have been since you were a child, which is why I won't allow it in the house."

"I cannot help it if young men send me posies," Lady Margaret shot back.

"After your cousin was arrested, your tears were true," I resolutely went on. "But when I first served you tea, before that event, you smelled strongly of jasmine, I assumed from perfume or cologne, but your tears then were your reaction to the plant, not genuine grief. When it occurred to me that you'd given yourself only the appearance of grief, I had to wonder why. Perhaps you hadn't been close to your brother but wanted to show sorrow at his passing, even if you felt none, so that your father would not be upset. But it was more likely to disguise the fact that you were indeed happy he was gone. Cousin Desmond had little money, Lady Cynthia told me, and he wasn't approved of for you. But if Lord Alfred and Desmond's older brother were to die, the trifling matter of money would be solved." I dared look directly at Lord Babcock. "Possibly you might die as well, begging your pardon, your lordship."

What made me saddest of all was that Lord Babcock did not seem surprised. His mouth turned down, and he appeared to age before my eyes. "I was a fool to indulge and spoil you," he said heavily to Lady Margaret. "I've always known that."

Lady Margaret shoved her chair back and sprang to her feet once more. "You cannot possibly believe her," she announced to the rest of the room. "That I stabbed my own brother with a kitchen knife? That is madness. *She* was in the hall with him." Lady Margaret pointed a trembling finger at Lady Babcock. "*She* took Mrs. Morgan the tea with the morphine in it Saturday, giving *her* plenty of time to steal a knife." The pointing finger switched to me. "I'm sorry Mrs. Morgan fell ill, and we had to have *this* terrible cook work for us, but it was my stepmother that gave our cook the tea."

"I never said the morphine was in the tea," I said quietly. "Or on what day it was served."

Color seeped into Lady Margaret's face in red blotches. "Stop this!" she shrieked, balling her hands. "You cannot possibly take the word of a *cook* over mine."

"Sit down." Again, Lord Babcock's voice rolled over his daughter's. "I worried it was you from the first, which is why I did not want the police here." He turned to Cynthia with a hint of pleading. "Margaret can't go to the magistrate. You can see that. I'd planned to deal with her myself—send her far away—but that decision was taken from me when Scotland Yard turned up."

Cynthia nodded, her face wan. "I have a chum whose father is something in the Home Office. I could have a word. See what he can do."

She meant her friend Miss Townsend, whose father was prominent in the ministry that oversaw the police departments. I'd never been certain what he did, but apparently, Mr. Townsend was quite powerful.

"I would be grateful," Lord Babcock answered. "For now, Margaret, you should confine yourself to your bedchamber."

"You know *she* did it." Lady Margaret pointed once more

to Lady Babcock, who sat in stoic perplexity. "If you search her chamber, you'll find the knife. _She_ killed your son, because she's an evil, evil woman." Tears, true ones, streamed down Lady Margaret's cheeks. "I only want to marry Desmond. *To marry Desmond ... "*

Her knees buckled as she trailed off. Cynthia hurried to catch her before she fell, Mrs. Seabrook rushing in again with the smelling salts.

Before either could reach her, Lady Margaret came to life, struck out at Cynthia, and then lunged at me.

I gazed into the eyes of a young woman who'd never been denied anything, who thought she could do what she pleased to obtain what she wanted, even something as heinous as killing her own brother.

I brought up my arm to fend off her blows. Lady Margaret managed to strike me twice before Mrs. Seabrook seized her around the waist and dragged her from me.

Margaret turned to the housekeeper and sagged in her arms, relapsing into tears. "Help me, Seabrook. Make them leave me alone."

"There now," Mrs. Seabrook's voice went surprisingly soft as she gathered Lady Margaret to her as though she were a child. "There now. It will be all right."

I wasn't certain how it could be, but at Mrs. Seabrook's words, Lady Margaret quieted. Mrs. Seabrook held her for a moment, stroking her back in its ill-fitting frock, then eased Lady Margaret out of the room, a supporting arm around her.

Lord Babcock's face was like stone. Losing both of his children in the space of a day must be a terrible blow. I had a daughter of my own, one I'd see this afternoon. If anything happened to Grace, it would break me.

"Go," Lord Babcock said to me before I could form any words of compassion. "Leave my house, where you have caused so much trouble. Cynthia, take her, and do not return yourself. That goes for your tedious aunt and uncle as well."

"Of course," Lady Cynthia answered. She was polite enough not to remind Lord Babcock she'd just offered to use her connections to lessen Lady Margaret's sentence. "Good afternoon, Lady Babcock, Miss Jordan." Cynthia nodded at them then ushered me to the door.

I sent a glance at Miss Jordan, who returned my look with a nod. The police probably would find the murder weapon in Lady Babcock's chamber, because Margaret, who'd been ensconced in that room most of yesterday afternoon, had the opportunity to hide it there. Miss Jordan, I surmised, would make certain the police knew Lady Babcock had nothing to do with that.

As Cynthia and I slid out, Lady Babcock rose and went to her husband. He remained stiff when she touched his arm and spoke quietly into his ear.

All at once, Lord Babcock transformed from the cold aristocrat to a father who'd never thought he'd have to face the things he had today. His mask dropped, and he turned to embrace his wife, his shoulders drooping.

I closed the door, and Cynthia and I moved quietly away.

When we left the house, Inspector McGregor, who had been waiting outside, gave Lady Cynthia a nod and me a more grudging one before he and Sergeant Scott approached the front door. Cynthia and I left them to it.

"Well, that was beastly," Cynthia declared as we trudged from Portman Square toward Oxford Street. A sudden wind struck us, as though trying to scour from us the sadness of the house we'd just departed.

"Yes," I agreed. "But if we had said nothing, Lady Margaret might not have stopped with Lord Alfred and Mrs. Morgan." I tried to feel high-minded about revealing her guilt, but I could not. I could only picture Lord Babcock collapsing in grief into his wife's arms.

Cynthia deflated. "I know. Ah, well, I'll be off to speak to Judith. Greet your little girl for me."

My heart lightened when I thought of Grace. She'd be waiting.

Cynthia and I parted, she heading to Upper Brook Street to visit Miss Townsend while I made my way toward the City and the house where my daughter dwelled.

As I strode along, the melancholy the house in Portman Square had settled on me began to ease, though it would leave its mark.

If Mrs. Bywater hadn't been the interfering busybody she was, I'd have only heard of the death of Lord Alfred in passing. I'd feel sorry for the family then return to my tasks, the event soon forgotten.

Then again, if Mrs. Bywater hadn't volunteered my services, Mrs. Morgan might be dead of too large a dose of morphine, and Lady Babcock might have been arrested for both murders. I'd done some good, I reminded myself. Also, for the first time in her life, Lady Margaret would have to answer for her misdeeds.

It would be a long time, however, before I forgot the cruel desperation in Lady Margaret's eyes and the acknowledgment on Lord Babcock's face that his choices in life had led, if indirectly, to the loss of both his children.

I drew a long breath as I walked, letting the spring breeze refresh me. It was a lesson, I decided, to balance love with responsibility, and to see that my daughter never had cause to despise or fear me. I would be as good to her as I possibly could, for now and for always.

My feet hurt by the time I reached Cheapside, as I'd been too distracted to seek an omnibus or a hansom. The ache receded as I turned to Clover Lane, where Grace lived with my dearest friends.

I felt a warmth at my side and started as Daniel fell into step with me and slid a firm hand through the crook of my arm.

I hadn't seen Daniel since he'd looked in on me early this morning to tell me he'd related all I'd told him to Inspector McGregor. The inspector had been most annoyed, of course, but he'd realized he had to release Cousin Desmond and had sourly sent the order.

I hadn't noticed Third Cousin Desmond rushing to Mount Street to assure Lady Margaret he was well. I wondered if he'd fled back to his home, wherever it was, to recover, and whether he'd already concluded what Lady Margaret had done.

"Your troubles are not allowed here," Daniel told me, scattering my thoughts. "The rest of the afternoon is for joy."

"Not joy," I quipped. "Grace."

Daniel's laughter rumbled, and with his strength beside me, I believed I could tackle anything.

My spirits lifted still more when Grace opened the door of the little house on Clover Lane and rushed out to me.

I caught my daughter in my arms, felt her kiss on my cheek, and absorbed her excited greeting. Daniel waited for us to finish our embrace, his eyes warm.

I was a woman blessed, I decided. I would savor this happiness for as long as I possibly could.

"That was a nice, squishy hug," Grace proclaimed when I

at last released her. "Let us go inside, and you can give Aunt Joanna a squishy hug too."

Daniel's laughter boomed, lighting the overcast day. I clasped Grace by one hand, Daniel with the other, and together we rushed into the house, laughter and sweetness floating on the April wind.

The Glass House

The Sudbury School Murders

The Necklace Affair

A Body in Berkeley Square

A Covent Garden Mystery

A Death in Norfolk

A Disappearance in Drury Lane

Murder in Grosvenor Square

The Thames River Murders

The Alexandria Affair

A Mystery at Carlton House

Murder in St. Giles

Death at Brighton Pavilion

The Custom House Murders

Murder in the Eternal City

A Darkness in Seven Dials

Murder on the Rhône

Leonidas the Gladiator Mysteries

(w/a Ashley Gardner)

Blood of a Gladiator

Blood Debts (novella)

A Gladiator's Tale

The Ring that Caesar Wore

Brother at Arms

ABOUT THE AUTHOR

New York Times, USA Today, and *Wall Street Journal* bestselling author Jennifer Ashley has more than 100 published novels and novellas in mystery, romance, historical fiction, and urban fantasy under the names Jennifer Ashley, Allyson James, and Ashley Gardner. Jennifer's books have been translated into more than a dozen languages and have earned starred reviews in *Publisher's Weekly* and *Booklist.* When she isn't writing, Jennifer enjoys playing music (guitar, piano, flute), reading, knitting, hiking, cooking, and building dollhouse miniatures.

More about Jennifer's books can be found at
http://www.jenniferashley.com
and
http://www.katholloway.com
To keep up to date on her new releases, join her newsletter here:
http://eepurl.com/47kLL

www.ingramcontent.com/pod-product-compliance
Lightning Source LLC
Chambersburg PA
CBHW031032310726
48969CB00007B/1957